This book is dedicated to my family,
who taught me the meaning of unconditional love.

ACKNOWLEDGEMENTS

There are so many people who helped me and inspired me to write this book. People say that writing is lonely but with the right people it really can be a very social experience. So, first and foremost, I would like to thank the Moore Street Masterminds: Fran, Lisa, Ayesha, Freja, Michelle, and our fabulous teacher and author Sophia Bennett. Without our weekly meetings at Michelle's house and coffee mornings at Foyles and our ongoing zoom meetings through the pandemic I never would have completed this novel.

I would also like to thank Brenda and Carmen for reading and giving constructive feedback on my chapters and all the fun times in the British Library and the City Lit café.

To my dear friends Claire and Kathy for taking the time to read my book and give me harsh but fair feedback, despite their crazy busy lives. I would also like to thank Khadija and Nadia who educated me about the hijab.

A huge thank you to Abiola Bello and Helen Lewis for taking a chance on my book and making my childhood dream of having a book published come true. You have been amazing and fabulous to work with.

I must thank my lovely sisters Sabiha, Semeen and Shireen, and my gorgeous Mum Shakila. We may have heated discussions, but no one can ever say our house is boring! I also want to thank my lovely nephews and nieces who keep me young and try to keep me up to date with all the latest teen slang.

I must also acknowledge the memory of my beloved father;

I still think about you every day and know you would be so proud of me.

I have to thank my beautiful kids Aneesa, Rafi and Saif, you guys keep me on my toes and help me remember what it was like to be a teen. Finally, I must thank my amazing husband Rehan. No girl could ever ask for a husband this supportive and tolerant, I could not have completed this book without you.

CHAPTER ONE

I fold the black scarf into a large triangle and the material feels smooth under my fingers.

Shafqat Aunty's suggestion of using viscose is good because the scarf doesn't slip as much. Staring at the mirror I drape my protective shield—my hijab—over my head, the right side hanging down on to my shoulder. I place the shorter end under my chin. Taking the long side, I wrap it behind my head, then pull it over to the left, fixing it into place with my silver sequinned pin, and see a solitary strand of hair poking out. I tuck it back under the scarf and smile at my reflection.

"Aisha, why you have to wear this thing all the time?" Mum asks, walking into my room. "Why you are making life harder for yourself?"

I know she's only worried about me, but her voice is so shrill the words practically ring in my ears. I remember all the fights Mum and I have had. She didn't want me to wear the hijab because she felt people would treat me differently and it could affect my chances of getting into university or getting a job. I might be picked on for the rest of my life, but I knew it was the right thing for me to do.

"I'm fine Mum, don't worry about it. Everyone's okay with it."

What she doesn't know won't hurt her, right? Mum gives me a disapproving look and I escape the house in a hurry.

It rained the whole Easter holidays, but now that we're going back to school it's sunny and warm. Typical. The leaves on the trees flutter in the wind and I smell freshly cut grass. Just thinking of the summer term makes me think of exams— year twelve exams! Things are getting serious. If I want to get out of Kent and move to London for university I really need to knuckle down. There's so much more diversity in London. At least there I won't feel out of place like I do here in school.

I'm waiting for the bus when I see two boys from the neighbouring school wearing scruffy grey uniforms, one fat with a shaved head, and one thin.

"Fancy a smoke?" the boy with the shaved head says, offering me one.

I'm nauseated by the stench of cigarette smoke as he leans towards me.

"I don't smoke."

"Is that cos you're a Moooslim? Your mummy and daddy and your Allah wouldn't like it." Shaved head has a deep, nasty voice.

"I don't want to, okay?" I turn away.

"Go on, you'll like it once you try it."

That's when I hear the skinny one whisper, "Pull her scarf off."

I've been bullied before, but no one's ever threatened to remove my scarf. My heart pounds and I shuffle backwards but there's nowhere left to go; I'm trapped against the back of the bus shelter. Other people at the bus stop turn their heads away. I instinctively put my hands to my hijab and pull the edges of the fabric towards me.

"Try it." Shaved head practically pushes the cigarette into my mouth. He stinks of B.O. I twist away and silently start praying to myself in Arabic.

"Qul ho wal a ho ahad—allah hoos samad lam ya lid wa lam u lud, was lam ya qul la hoo kofo one ahad."

I can't remember exactly what it means word for word, but I know it's a prayer to protect you from bad things.

As the boys tower over me, I start shaking, my legs like jelly as though I'm sinking into the ground, like it's turned to quicksand. Suddenly, a hand appears over shaved head's shoulders, grasps his wrist, and yanks it away from my face.

"She said no, okay?" a male voice says forcefully.

At first, the sunlight in my eyes made my saviour seem like a huge, invincible shadow-creature, but now I see that he's a tall, dark-haired boy with floppy hair. He pulls shaved head by his arm, forcing him to step away from me.

"Alright, mate, I got it, I'll leave her alone!"

Dark-haired boy lets go of his arm.

"What the hell? Hang out with terrorists if you want," the skinny boy shouts as he backs away.

"Get out of here!" dark-haired boy shouts, and the two boys scuttle away to the other side of the bus stop.

"Thank you." I stare down at my shoes. I don't want him to see the few tears that have escaped from my eyes.

"I'm Darren by the way. I just moved here from London. What's your name?"

I look up and Darren smiles at me. For a second, my

breath catches in my throat as I stare transfixed into his hazel eyes. They're so dreamlike I could almost dive into them. My heart rate quickens. He's tall and dressed smartly in black trousers with a white shirt and grey blazer. Not quite school uniform but formal.

"I'm Aisha."

Thank you for helping me; thank you for not thinking like them, is what I want to say, but I can't seem to get the words out.

"Do you know Forest High? I'm gonna be in the sixth form there."

Aah, no wonder he's dressed smartly; it's school policy that sixth formers dress how they would for the world of work.

"No way, I go there! I'm in sixth form too." I grin at him.

"Is it any good? What are the teachers like?"

I frown. "Well, it depends on what you're studying."

"History, chemistry, and physics."

Handsome *and* clever.

"That's some tough subjects. What do you want to do?"

"I want to be a human rights lawyer."

Wow, caring too.

"How comes you left London?"

Darren's smile vanishes. He swallows and stares at the floor with a frown. "I'm. . . it's complicated."

I wonder what's wrong? I want to ask but I don't want him to think I'm pushy. Luckily, the bus arrives before it becomes even more awkward.

Darren sits next to me once we've clambered aboard. I've sat next to boys before during class projects and stuff, but I've never felt so nervous. It's like I'm so aware of everything—the shine on my nose, the tiny hole in my tights, the way I can't stop my hands from fidgeting. Why have I never thought about how to talk to boys before? To be honest, the only boys I've really talked to are my annoying younger brothers and he certainly isn't like them. He must think I'm so nervous and weird.

"Is it always like that?" Darren asks. "I mean with the bullying and stuff."

"Yeah, sometimes, but no one's ever threatened to rip my scarf off before."

"That's so bad. Have you told anyone about this?"

I feel my skin prickle. I hate the way he's looking at me with pity.

"It's not that simple, you know," I eventually say.

"I bet it's really difficult."

"Maybe I should stand up for myself more? Toughen up? But they're the ones with the problem, not me. Why do I have to change?"

Darren's face flushes. "No, of course you're right. You don't have to change who you are. A lot of my friends from my old school wore the hijab. The girls were pretty feisty and no one dared mess with them, but everyone's different. I'm just glad I was there to help you. Those guys were total losers."

"Thank you," I say.

He's so lovely. I wonder why he's being so nice to me. He smiles and I notice a little scar by his left eye. I focus on the scar and try not to think about how handsome he is with those ridiculously beautiful eyes that seem to pierce right through to my soul.

I look away. I'm not meant to notice things like that.

CHAPTER TWO

"You do realise that new boy hasn't stopped staring at you," Isabelle whispers during chemistry.

Isabelle Fleming has been my best friend since year seven, when we both had braces and scraped back hair. Now she wears her gorgeous brown hair long and bone straight. She has killer cheekbones, a slim frame, and her skirts are always very short, skin-tight, and just about adhering to the school policy of smart dress.

I'm always in black trousers, white shirt, black hijab. We couldn't look more different, but we're still best friends. We have a secret that no one else knows—we're both really into Taylor Swift and Harry Styles. If anyone found that out about Isabelle, she would so lose her street cred. I often joke with her that she should never ditch me because I can totally blackmail her with this information whereas I don't think anyone would be in the least bit interested or surprised to know that I still love them, especially Harry.

I'm blushing. I know she means Darren is staring at me as he's the only new boy in school. He's sitting by the window a few rows back. Our desks are in pairs and we both cast a furtive glance backwards. It's true, he's staring in our direction. I drop my gaze and try to focus on the equations on my page.

"He's gorgeous." She giggles.

"Are you sure he's not staring at you?" I ask. "You're way better looking than me."

Let's face facts: she *is* a lot prettier than me, and she's allowed to date, unlike me.

"Oh, that's not true." Isabelle brushes me off, but I know she's only saying that to be nice. She pushes her hair behind her ear and flashes me a conniving grin. "Let's go and chat to him after class."

I nod, ignoring my thoughts which are racing at a million miles per hour.

In true Isabelle fashion, as soon as class ends, she drags me by the hand to talk to Darren. He's standing by the lockers right next to the chemistry lab. It's always busy around here and there's not enough room for me to edge in next to them, so I stand awkwardly to the side and resign myself to getting jostled by kids running between lessons.

"So, what do you think of our school?" Isabelle asks. "Do you like Kent?"

Darren shrugs. "It's pretty I suppose but it kind of sucks cos I don't know anyone here—all my mates are in London."

"And your girlfriend, I bet," Isabelle says.

She is so not subtle.

Darren looks right at me and says, "I don't have a girlfriend."

Why did he look at me? Did Isabelle notice?

"Great! I mean no one will mind if you come to my party Friday night then," Isabelle says.

"Will you be there, Aisha?" Darren asks.

I shake my head.

Isabelle elbows him, so he focuses back on her, and bats her long lashes at him.

"Aisha doesn't come to parties," she says in her sweet flirty voice.

And I wish more than anything that I could go. I glance at the clock in the hallway; it's time for Zuhr lunchtime prayer.

"I need to go and pray," I say. "I'll catch you guys later."

I walk down the corridor towards the prayer room knowing I shouldn't like that Darren was so focused on me, except I kinda do. I'm not really supposed to notice boys and, to be honest, it hasn't really been a problem for ages. Not since my last crush, aged fourteen, on my cousin in Pakistan where nothing much could happen because our only line of communication was Instagram.

I'm almost at the prayer room when I feel a tap on my shoulder. I turn around to find Darren standing in front of me.

"Don't you want to come to the party? You don't have to drink, you know, if that's what you're worried about."

Another kid walks past us slowly in the corridor. From the corner of my eye, I see him gazing at us and I know he's thinking, what's this short girl in a hijab doing with this tall, good-looking guy?

"I don't go to parties, Darren."

"But you want to come, don't you? I'm sure we could find an excuse to tell your parents if they're strict. You could say we have a study group."

"You want me to lie to my parents?" I raise my eyebrows.

"The girls from my old school, they all had to make up stuff so they could go out. It's not a big deal."

Not all Muslims are the same, I want to say, but I don't. I know he's only trying to be nice.

"I don't want to go to parties; I don't want to smoke or drink. No one is making me wear this scarf." Mum and Dad's nagging faces pop into my mind. "Especially my parents. They would prefer it if I took it off. Look, I really need to go and pray."

I turn to go before he says something else stupid, but then he blurts out, "Can I have your number?"

He wants my number?! Why on earth does he want my number? Oh my God, what do I do? Does he fancy me? No, it can't be that, maybe he just wants to be friends? After all, he is new to the area. I turn back around.

"You can have my number but I'm not going to change my mind."

He hands me his phone and I type in the digits.

"I'm texting you mine," he says.

A second later my phone buzzes in my coat pocket. "I've really got to go," I say.

He nods but he doesn't move. I turn and walk away but I can feel his eyes boring into the back of my head. I can't understand why my stomach's turning somersaults and my face feels like it's burning. I need to pray and ask Allah for guidance.

CHAPTER THREE

When I wake the next day, I'm shaking. I'm dreading going to the bus stop—what if those boys are there again? I secretly hope that Darren will be around to save me from any more trouble. I leave it till the last minute practically dragging my feet all the way.

When I get to the bus stop, the bullies from yesterday are there too and my stomach twists, but then I see Darren fiddling with his phone. I notice that he has gelled his hair back today. He looks up and waves. Was he waiting for me?

The boys from yesterday seem to be standing a million miles away from Darren and don't say anything, although they do keep sneering and smirking at us.

"Hey, Aisha," Darren greets me with a warm smile on his face which makes his eyes light up. The hair off his face today draws more attention to those hazel pools of deliciousness

Stop it, Aisha. Stop checking him out.

"Did you just get here?" I ask.

"I've been here for about ten minutes," he replies. "I was waiting for you."

What? He *was* waiting for me.

"I didn't want you to have to deal with those idiots again."

He glances in the direction of the bullies, and they quickly look away.

I want to say something along the lines of, "Oh my God, that's the nicest thing anyone has ever done for me," but instead I just nod and gulp to keep the nerves at bay.

"That one on the left, he looks like such a weasel," he continues. "Like he's the fat kid's slave, don't you think?"

"Totally!" I laugh.

I can tell that he has sensed how nervous I am and is trying to put me at ease, and it's working. I'm already feeling more relaxed. He has this deep rich voice that reminds me of melted caramel.

"You never told me what subjects you're doing," Darren says.

"Chemistry, history and maths."

"Maybe we'll have history together too. I was chuffed when I realised you were in my chemistry class."

Wow, he's already planning what lessons we share; I'm taken aback by how direct he is. I secretly hope we do have the same class though. A buzz of excitement runs through me at the thought of sitting next to him.

"So, what do you want to be, a doctor or something?"

He clearly knows the Asian stereotypes.

"I don't know," I say. "My parents would love that, but I'd really like to do a history degree or something. Pretty geeky, huh?"

He shrugs. "No, it's cool. History is my weakest subject so I respect anyone who can write those long essays properly. You must be pretty smart."

I blush.

"You should tutor me or something." He laughs.

"I'd have to charge, you know," I say, smiling.

The bus arrives, and we have such a laugh on the journey. He wants to know all the dirt about the school staff, so I tell him about the chemistry teacher.

"She seems super-scary," he says. "Like she could shoot lasers from her eyes."

"I know, right, she's like a total dragon lady. We're all petrified of her," I say. "By the way, what do you think of the lab technician?"

"Who's that? The weird guy with the mental weave and those mad coked-up eyes? The one who keeps dropping all the burettes and smashing them?"

"Yes!" I laugh so hard I have to put my hand over my mouth. "I couldn't have described him better myself."

"I don't even know why I'm doing chemistry. I want to be a human rights lawyer, so God knows what help it will be."

"That's so cool. Do you do a lot of stuff for charity then?" I ask.

He shakes his head. "I should, right? Apart from anything, I need something to put on the UCAS form. Do you?"

"Yeah, when I can," I say, and leave it at that.

I don't elaborate on the weekends I've spent helping out at soup kitchens and charity shops, cooking food for the homeless. I don't want to sound like I'm showing off.

"I do want to get into charity work, though. I've been on quite a few marches and protests, you know, campaigning for human rights."

"Really?" I'm intrigued now.

"Well, the latest was this anti-racism march in London. It

was brilliant, and in my old school I kind of ran the Amnesty International group. We did a lot of fundraising and stuff through that, but I don't think it really counts as charity work."

This guy is impressive. It's not just what he says, it's the passion behind how he says it. His gravelly voice makes him seem so much more mature than any of the boys I've met at our school. My face aches from smiling so much.

He's staring at me intensely as if I'm the most important person in the world. My palms feel sweaty. There's this weird energy in the air. I'm not used to anyone, let alone a good-looking guy, giving me this kind of attention. It's like the sun is shining only on me and I feel almost out of breath.

"So why are you doing chemistry, then?" I say quickly. "I mean if it doesn't help your career choice?"

"My dad, he's all like science gives you an edge—dunno what the hell that's about." He sighs. "To be honest, all I really want to do is play football or tennis, not study all the time."

"So, you're the sporty type?"

Sporty people make me nervous—they always seem so confident and in their element and I have no idea what that's like.

"I suppose so. I play football—I was on the team at my old school, and I'll probably join the team here too. But I'm also a bit of a tennis nerd. I'm obsessed with Wimbledon."

"How come?"

"Mum—she brainwashed me with it. At least that's what my dad always says, he thinks tennis is girly and the only sport for boys is football." A sour expression comes over his face.

"Parents are like that," I say. "They always have such fixed ideas about everything."

"Tell me about it." He rolls his eyes but then gives me this sweet smile and I can't help but drop my gaze. The weird energy is still there.

In school, I don't see him all day but can't stop thinking about the way he looked at me and how it made me feel warm all over. I can't seem to get that look off my mind. I can't stop thinking how sexy his voice is and how kind and caring he seems. I can't stop thinking about him.

If only he was a Muslim.

At lunchtime, everyone is talking about Isabelle's party. It seems like everyone is going—except me. I stand in line with my sad little tray and see Isabelle near the front, laughing and chatting with the popular kids. I should just go over and join them, but I'm always so shy and awkward and these confident kids intimidate me.

Two girls called Ella and Susie are behind me. Susie has wire-rimmed glasses and mousy-brown hair, and Ella is a strawberry blonde with terrible acne but pretty, blue eyes. They are both in my chemistry class and are always nice to me.

"You can sit with us if you want," Susie says balancing her tray on one hand while she pushes up her glasses with the other.

"Thanks," I smile back. I can't stop looking at Isabelle and her cool friends.

Isabelle catches my eye. She gives me a warm, almost guilty smile, and motions me over. "Aisha, come up here and join us."

"It's okay, I'm going to sit with Ella and Susie," I say.

Isabelle makes her way down the line and grabs my arm. "No, you're not, come and sit with us. You're my friend. Ella and Susie, you can have her some other time."

I don't have much choice as she's already dragging me back with her. I glance behind me and mouth, '*sorry*' at the girls. They shrug in response.

The kids in front of me don't seem to mind that I push in. Isabelle puts her arm around me and whispers, "Why would you want to have lunch with them when you can be hanging with the cool kids?"

I can see Jason looking at me and Isabelle with narrowed eyes. I bet he's wondering why the hell Isabelle hangs out with me. But Isabelle and I have been friends forever and I know she would never dump me.

CHAPTER FOUR

It's Friday night and I'm stuck at home. I feel like Cinderella, left behind with only the mice to keep her company, or in my case my family.

I've been laying on my bed for over an hour. The light in my room is terrible. Dad still hasn't fixed the flickering bulb, and the horrible brown curtains Mum chose don't help either—they block out so much natural light. My scarf's on the floor next to three days' worth of unwashed socks.

I squint at my phone trying to check for messages. Swipe. Swipe. Swipe. It's never worked properly since my dumb little brother Burhan threw it at my even dumber brother Farhan. The screen looks like a glass spider web, and I can just about read through the cracks. Mum and Dad are refusing to pay for a new phone because they say if I'd bought a phone case, the screen wouldn't have smashed. They don't blame my brothers at all. Meh!

There are more than a dozen new Instagram posts from Isabelle looking amazing in her skimpy red dress. They've all gone out for drinks before the party. For a minute, I wonder how I would look in a dress like that; I'm curvier than she is, but I reckon I could pull it off. I wonder what Darren would think if he saw me dressed like that. Ugh, here I am thinking about him again. I keep looking at the pictures. I don't want to admit it to myself, but I'm looking for pictures of him.

I wish I were at the party. But even if Mum and Dad had let me go, what would I do there? It'd be so awkward standing around in a pub with my hijab on, surrounded by people drinking alcohol and not being able to join in.

I haven't seen any pictures of Darren yet—maybe he isn't there. I can't help feeling relieved. I look at Isabelle's friends' list, and see that Darren is already one of her friends and they're following each other. His profile picture is to die for. He's looking directly at the camera with those huge puppy dog eyes, his hair gelled back, wearing a jacket and a checked shirt. He has an intense dreamlike expression on his face and just a hint of that warm smile. I try pressing on his picture to see if I can see his story, but nothing happens. His account is private so I can't look at any of his posts or pictures—probably for the best. The constant checking is driving me crazy, and my phone is on ten percent, so I plug it into the charger and go downstairs.

"Aisha, come help me chop bhindi."

Even after years of living in England, Mum still speaks broken English. I kind of love how her English seems wrong but right at the same time. She sits at her usual place at the kitchen table wearing a faded green shalwar kameez, wire-framed glasses, and her favourite rattan chappals, so worn away that her toes are escaping from their wicker jail.

The windows are shut and always have been—my family fears ventilation—and the yellow, red, and brown stains on the walls reflect the aromas escaping from the bubbling pots.

When I was younger, if someone had been mean to me at school, Mum would give me a samosa and it would make my whole day better. Her samosas are the best.

"Do I have to?" I plead.

"Chopping or studying?"

I pause. I definitely can't focus on homework right now.

I sit down and Mum gives me a massive handful of thick green okra. Shafqat Aunty always calls them Ladies' Fingers, which I found hilarious when I was little. I hold the ends and begin chopping.

"You cut them too thick. They will not be crispy unless you cut them fine—good thing you are not planning to be a surgeon."

"That's right, Mum, I'm not."

What is it with so many Asians always wanting their kids to be doctors? It's like there's no other respectable profession—first a doctor and if that fails, a dentist or a pharmacist. God forbid if you want to do something arty or creative. I want to be an academic in history, but an Asian female professor in an arts subject won't do. Who would do the cooking and cleaning? At least that seems to be my family's view anyway.

I continue to chop and try hard to judge the thickness right without slicing my fingers. From the corner of my eye, I can see Mum staring at me.

"You look so pretty without your hijab . . ."

Normally a comment like that would annoy me, another ploy for her to persuade me to get rid of the scarf. Mum is convinced that living in Kent and wearing a hijab is asking for trouble. I would normally argue with her but today I'm interested in what she has to say. If she thinks

I'm good-looking, maybe other people would too. . . like Darren, even.

"What do you mean?"

"You have really pretty brown eyes, but with your hijab, people cannot see how nice they look with your thick brown hairs, especially when you comb them down." My cheeks flush. "I know you're a bit dark but that's because of your father. It's really not your fault that you'll never be fair like me."

And there it is, the usual snide comment. Why is it that Mum and all her friends are so obsessed with fair skin? I swear, you could be the most beautiful girl in the world but if you're a little bit dark, you're written off.

"Mum, not all this again about dark skin," I tut. "Don't you remember that time we were in Pakistan and there was that white woman in the market?"

"Yes, yes, the pretty lady," she replies.

"She was not pretty, Mum," I say. "You guys were all over her because she was fair-skinned. You're such a victim of colonialism."

"Okay, okay, forget about that woman," Mum says waving her hand at me. "I want to ask you something: why you don't take off your hijab for the function tomorrow? I want my friends to see what a pretty girl you've become."

"It doesn't work like that, Mum, you know that. What was the point of sending us to Islamic school for so many years when you don't follow what they teach us?"

Years ago, Mum and Dad would drag us out of bed every Sunday, push us into our old Toyota Corolla, and drive for miles to take us to a dusty, overheated front room in a terraced house. For three hours we would sit and recite the Qur'an and listen to Islamic stories about how to be a good Muslim.

We learned how to pray and that was where I met Shafqat Aunty, the kindest, sweetest woman I've ever met. She was the one who supported me in wearing the hijab. It was Shafqat Aunty who made me realise that there was no choice in the matter. Was I a Muslim or not? If I saw myself as a Muslim, then I should wear the hijab with pride as a symbol of my modesty and to show the world I was proud of my religion.

When I think about all the Muslims on TV and how some people think we're all bombers and terrorists, I wish I could introduce them to her. Maybe they'd change their minds.

I realise that Mum hasn't spoken for a while. The only noise I can hear is the sound of the knives hitting the wooden boards as we chop away.

Mum swallows and takes a deep breath. "We sent you so we can make connections with other Pakistani people. I come from Pakistan. I didn't know anyone here apart from your father and his besharam family." Besharam means shameless; Mum never has anything nice to say when it comes to Dad's family. "I came to England when I was nineteen, speaking no English. But with no experience I got a job in a factory, sewing. Making these connections will help for getting you married and things like that."

Married? Why is she thinking about that?

"Mum, can I ask you something?" I say carefully. "Did you ever think maybe you wouldn't have an arranged marriage, and that you'd meet someone and fall in love?"

As I say the words, the image of Darren smiling at me

at the bus stop pops into my mind and I try desperately to bat it away.

She laughs. "Of course I did! My friends and I had dream that we will meet some handsome millionaire, and he will ask me out for coffee and then ask me to marry him."

What? Really? I can't believe this is Mum talking.

"And did you ever meet anyone like that?" I ask.

There's a long pause.

"Of course not, I marry your father and come to England and all my dreams come true."

And then she laughs as if she has made the funniest joke ever.

I chop up the last bhindi and pick off the small green bits which have collected on my fingers. I walk towards the stairs.

"Where you are going?" Mum asks.

"I'm going to wash my hands."

"Well, why you do not do it here?"

"I feel like going upstairs."

I'm a liar. I want—no, I *need* to check my phone again. After washing my hands, I creep into my bedroom. I can't find a towel, so I dry my hands on the duvet cover. My mobile's charging on my bedside table; it's been about an hour since I last checked it. Why do I feel nervous? I look at it and am disappointed there are no messages for me, not from Isabelle or Darren.

I open Instagram, and there it is: a picture of Darren and Isabelle with her arm around him. Noo! My breathing is shallow and I'm burning up. I can't look at this. I switch off the phone, so the picture disappears as the screen goes black. All I see now are the web-like cracks covering the surface.

CHAPTER FIVE

Hanging out with a bunch of middle-aged women is not really my idea of fun, but today is different because we are at Shafqat Aunty's house. She isn't my real aunty, but every one of Mum's friends is referred to as Aunty because they are older. Shafqat Aunty wears the hijab like me.

Two years ago, when I was fifteen, I told her that I was reading about the hijab online and an article mentioned that it's compulsory for women to wear it once they hit puberty. I told her it was something I wanted to do to show my commitment to my religion, but I still had some doubts. I mean, wasn't it kind of sexist? But Shafqat Aunty has such a good way of explaining things.

"It depends how you interpret it. Some people say it is the opposite of sexist because you aren't viewed as an object. How you look is taken out of the equation and it's all about what you say and how you present yourself to the world. It's about identifying yourself as a Muslim."

This had totally swung it for me. As far as I was concerned, I was a feminist for wearing it. She had convinced Mum and Dad, and although they weren't happy, they accepted it. It's true, it has changed my life. People do stare at me, and all that stuff at the bus stop has begun, but I figure it's because in the area where we live it's so rare to see people wearing hijab, although I know it's common in London.

I go to my wardrobe and stare at the rows of salwar kameezes. Mum is always nagging me to look nice and I decide to take her advice for a change. Just because I wear a headscarf doesn't mean I'm invisible. I pick one out before I go to my parents' bedroom door. Mum has been in there for hours doing her makeup.

"What you are going to wear?" she asks.

"This!" I show her the red salwar kameez. The stiff chiffon material crackles as I glide across the room to her dressing table. The long tunic flows in deep pleats to my feet, which are enclosed in my best gold chappals. I wear a matching red hijab.

"Finally, you are taking an interest in your appearance! There is hope for you yet."

When we arrive at Shafqat Aunty's house, I'm scared to look at anyone. I wonder if anyone will notice the change in my appearance, like the black eyeliner highlighting my brown eyes and the faintest touch of blusher on my cheeks, but I am more frightened that they won't.

"Aisha," cries my friend Farhana. "Assalamualaikum! I haven't seen you in the longest time, you look lovely."

"So do you," I say, giving her a cuddle.

Farhana is gorgeous with perfect eye makeup. Her long black hair has golden highlights; it's glossy and snakes down her back. How can I compete with girls like these? My mood soon lifts when I see Shafqat Aunty.

Shafqat Aunty is a middle-aged woman, slightly overweight

with a baby-face. Her cheeks sag, but they're soft, and she has the kindest face. She wears a brown salwar kameez with gold wire embellishments, and her hair is covered with a black hijab.

"Aisha!" Shafqat Aunty exclaims. "You've grown so much, you look wonderful Ma'Shallah."

"Thank you, Aunty," I say.

She leads me to the living room. All the chairs have been pushed against the wall, and the carpet is covered with a crisp white sheet.

I say, "Assalamualaikum" to the other ladies who stare at me and smile.

Some of them squeeze my cheeks as if I were still six. I go to the pile of Siparas, or chapters from the Qur'an, take one, sit on a soft cushion on the floor and begin to read in Arabic—I don't really know what the words mean but I read them anyway.

We're here because one lady's husband is having bypass surgery and the prayers are to help him. To be honest, I'm not really thinking about any of that while I'm reading. I can't stop thinking about Darren. Has something happened between him and Isabelle already? I can't get that picture out of my head and I really want to speak to Shafqat Aunty. Ever since I met Darren, I feel like he's on my mind all the time and I don't know what to do with these feelings. Why is he always popping into my brain? I must stop thinking about him.

Shafqat Aunty is so busy though. After we finish reading Qur'an, there are the prayers and songs, and she is leading all of that. Then there's lunch, and I go to the kitchen to help in the hope that I'll be able to speak to her then, but it's too busy and before I know it, I'm spending ages ladling out daal and pilau rice, desperately trying to make sure nothing falls on my salwar kameez. I'm not sure I'll ever get to talk to her.

"You're such a good girl, Aisha," Shafqat Aunty says every so often. She squeezes my cheek now and then, but somehow when she does it, it's not irritating.

Finally, people start leaving and I think I may have my chance to talk to her, but then Mum says she wants to leave too.

"But I need to talk to Shafqat Aunty."

"About what?" Mum narrows her eyes. She always questions what I speak to Aunty about. I'm convinced she's jealous of our relationship.

"Oh, just some Islam stuff. I want her advice," I say.

Mum stares at me then says, "Okay, I talk to my friends then, but be quick because I have a lot to do at home."

I find Shafqat Aunty finally sitting on the sofa. She is massaging her feet and looks tired. Maybe, now is not the right time.

She notices me and waves me over. "Come, Aisha, sit with me." Her soft face beams with a warm smile. "I want to thank you so much for all your hard work. Today, you worked even harder than Zeba."

Luckily, her daughter is out of earshot, but I can't help blushing with pride. She considers me better than her own daughter! This is my chance.

"Aunty do you ever worry about things?"

"Of course," she says. "Everyone does, but what sort of things do you mean?"

"You know that perhaps you miss out on a lot by being religious and maybe it would be better, easier, to just get rid of the hijab?"

"Why are you saying this, Aisha? What's happened?"

She leans forward and puts her arms around me. I want so much to tell her everything—that I've met a guy and I like him, and maybe I'm crazy, but I think he likes me too, but it's all wrong because I'm not meant to be thinking about things like that and why is it stressing me out so much? Why can't I stop thinking about him all the time? But I don't know if she will understand, and I don't want her to be disappointed in me.

"It's so hard being the only Muslim in school."

"Are they still being nasty to you?" she asks and squeezes me close to her. "Those mean boys?"

"Aunty, it's not only them, it's everyone." Suddenly I feel my eyes welling up. I pick up the napkin to wipe the flood of tears that I now can't control. "Only the other day I was in the post office and the lady behind the counter was so rude to me. She was nice to all the other customers. I only wanted to buy some stamps and she practically threw them at me and kept telling me to stand aside when I wanted to write the address on my letter and give it to her to weigh. The way she spoke to me was like I was something dirty on her shoe. I'm sure it was because of the hijab. This stuff never happened to me before I started wearing it."

Shafqat Aunty doesn't say anything, she keeps holding me close to her and we take it in turns to wipe away my tears. After what seems like the longest time she says very softly, "This is why you must pray and keep your faith in Allah. What you are describing is Shaitan trying to lead you astray."

She squeezes my hand kindly. "Sometimes Allah tests us to try to bring us closer to him. He makes things difficult for us so that we remember him. We must turn to Allah in tough times. You are planning to fast, aren't you? Ramadan starts next week. You will see that fasting gives you clarity of mind, and strength, and these feelings, they will disappear."

I nod. I know I've chickened out of telling Shafqat Aunty the truth, but she's still made me feel better. I'm going to fast, learn self-control, and forget all about Darren. I won't think about him anymore.

CHAPTER SIX

The alarm goes at three fifteen am and I can hear Mum scrambling about.

"Wake up, Aisha, it's time for Suhoor," she shouts.

It's the first day of Ramadan and we must eat before the sun rises. Mum comes into my room and switches on the light. I scrunch my eyes and force myself to sit up.

"How much time's left?" I ask.

"About fifteen minutes, come on, get up."

It's a real struggle but I force myself up and drag myself to the bathroom. I catch sight of my brothers fast asleep in their bed—Burhan on the top bunk and Farhan on the lower bunk. I'm so jealous that they get to sleep because they're too young to fast.

Bleary-eyed, I brush my teeth then make my way downstairs. The kitchen feels eerie at this time of the morning. Usually, you can hear cars zooming past the windows, but it's pitch black and silent. Mum has set the table, and on top of the flowery tablecloth covered by a thick plastic sheet lining, there is a meat curry, paratha, plus egg and toast, and a cup of tea waiting for me.

"Mum, it's quarter past three in the morning, I can't eat so much. I only want a banana and a glass of milk."

"You have to eat; you will become tired during the day," Mum insists.

I force the paratha down with a bit of egg but it's a real struggle. The paratha is greasy, and I find that my fingers are covered in oil which I wipe on the edge of the tablecloth when Mum is looking the other way. I watch Mum and Dad shovelling the food down like there's no tomorrow. How can they do that without being sick? Dad's bald head looks extra shiny in this light. I notice bits of egg yolk sticking to his moustache, and shudder inwardly.

We glance up at the clock: it's three thirty am. Nearly time for sunrise; we're not allowed to eat once we can see daylight.

"Time to stop eating," says Mum. "Ramadan Mubarak. Right, I'm off to bed."

"But what about Fajr? We have to wait to pray, Mum."

"I'm too tired and your dad has to go to work early in the morning. We'll do it later—you should do it later too—you have school," Mum says.

I make my way upstairs to my bedroom. I'm wide awake now and will wait to say my dawn prayers. What's the point of fasting if you aren't going to pray? Or maybe she's right—I will only be making myself more tired. What if I turn up at school with bags under my eyes? What will Darren think of me then? I shake my head. Stop thinking about him.

I check my messages on my phone. There's one from Shafqat Aunty wishing me Ramadan Mubarak.

I text back.

ME: *Shafqat Aunty, Ramadan Mubarak—Mum says I should go to sleep now but I think I should pray Fajr, what do you think?*

I know she won't answer straight away so I head off to the bathroom to make wudu.

There's something therapeutic and soothing about the sound of the water and the ritualistic way in which I must clean myself before praying. The repetition, the one-two-three-pattern, as I wash my hands and face and feet, somehow clears my mind of whirring thoughts. Darren can wait. My prayers must come first.

My prayer mat, the Ja Namaz, is stored on a shelf, its fringed edge hanging over the side. I take it down and unfold it. Lines have marked it from being pressed into a square so many times. I begin my prayers, and it seems this is the most focused I have been for ages.

Today is special. I must make every act of worship count.

The yellow carpeted rug feels soft under my bare feet, although part of it is threadbare from being used so many times. There's a symmetrical picture of a black wedge-like cube in the middle, the Ka'ba, with pillars on either side. A strange blue two-dimensional garden is pictured underneath it, which sort of plays tricks on your eyes because of the lack of perspective.

I must have perspective. I must stay focused. I must not let my thoughts wander to Darren.

The repetition, the rhythm feels soothing. While my lips speak Arabic in my mind, I keep internally begging Allah to look after me and keep me strong.

Help me Allah, help me to stop feeling like this.

The first streaks of grey wash across the canvas of the sky.

What will today bring? Will I see him? I won't think about him. Not even a little bit.

Doing the Fajr prayer so early in the morning feels great. I can face the day and resist everything. I know I can. There will be no thoughts of Darren today.

Getting back to sleep at four am, however, is hard. I'm wide awake and already thirsty. I check my messages again, and Shafqat Aunty has answered.

SHAFQAT AUNTY: *Aisha of course you should pray Fajr! Good luck for your first fast. Remember this is a very special and powerful month. It will be easy to fast if you remember that fasting in Ramadan is to cleanse our minds and our bodies. It's a chance to really begin afresh, to have all our sins forgiven. Remember you were asking how to deal with difficult thoughts. May our steadfastness and patience during Ramadan show us the way and lead us together on the path of peace and harmony.*

ME: *Ramadan Mubarak! Shafqat Aunty x*

I smile, feeling at peace I let my eyes shut, and I drift off to sleep.

When I wake in the morning, though, I'm in a cold sweat, I'm shaking. My heart is thudding; I feel like my chest might burst with the intensity of my palpitations.

Darren, Darren, Darren, I'm mouthing his name without even realising it.

Despite my prayers, I dreamt about him the whole night, but I can't quite remember all the details. I think I was just about to break my fast and he was sitting next to me at the kitchen table, ready to pass me a juicy date. He fed me the date and then he passed me a glass of water to moisten my lips. My lips were glistening and pink, and so were his. I try to remember what happened next, but I can't quite recall. I know he leaned into me, those hazel eyes locked on mine. He was so close, and I think he was going to kiss me—that must have been when I woke up. The guilt I feel is overwhelming, but so is the feeling of disappointment. Why did the dream have to end there? Why couldn't it have ended after he kissed me?

CHAPTER SEVEN

"Coming to the tuck shop?" Isabelle asks at break time. "I have to tell you about my weekend with Darren."

I freeze. Did she say weekend? Why are they spending the weekend together?

I hesitate; should I tell her that I started my fast today? People round here don't really know much about fasting. This is my first year of doing it at school, and I've never really talked to Isabelle about it before. She'll probably think it's weird or it'll make her feel uncomfortable like she can't eat around me, but I really want to know what happened with Darren. I feel my throat tightening and lick my already dry lips.

I nod and we make our way down the corridors to the tiny room that's the tuck shop. There's already a long line and Isabelle taps her feet impatiently and keeps telling me how hungry she is. I see the rows of chocolate bars and packets of crisps, and my stomach starts to rumble. The Kit-Kat seems to be staring at me. I toy with the idea of buying it and keeping it for later, but I don't want to think about it all day and smell it in my bag. I try to ignore the feeling that perhaps the pit in my stomach isn't just hunger.

Isabelle doesn't seem to notice that I don't buy anything. She buys a packet of crisps and a carton of orange juice, and we go outside and sit at one of the trestle tables scattered around. I needn't have worried about making her uncomfortable; she eats her crisps and sucks at her carton of drink, and luckily doesn't offer me either so no long explanations of fasting are needed.

"So, what happened with Darren?" I ask, trying not to sound too interested.

"Oh my God! He is so gorgeous. He came to the party late, and was so shy, I totally had to look after him. I introduced him, and everyone said we would make a great looking couple."

"You're together?" I try to ignore what feels like needles stabbing me in the chest.

"Well strictly speaking, we're not actually together yet," she says, her cheeks flushed. "We only had a goodbye cuddle, but I'm working on it. I was thinking of asking him to the cinema this weekend, you know snuggle up in the back seats and all that."

The idea of them in the back row cuddled up together, sends a sudden feeling of nausea washing over me.

"I reckon it's only a matter of time before we kiss. Anyway, he's going to have lunch with us today so tell me what you think, if you think he's into me or not."

Of course he's into her. Everyone is always into Isabelle. Why would someone like Darren be interested in someone as shy and unconfident as me?

"It sounds like he is," I say, and Isabelle beams. "Anyway, I might not come to lunch today."

"You have to!" she says. "When I asked him to lunch, he specifically asked if you'd be there. You two ride the bus together, right? Please, Aisha, I'm really nervous, I need you there. Please do it for me—you're my best friend." She squeezes my hand.

He specifically asked if you'd be there.

Why would he want me to be there if he's hanging out with Isabelle now?

"Alright I'll come."

I'm so confused, what is Darren playing at? Why does he want me to see them together? Is he trying to make me jealous?

I'm getting a headache and I don't feel well. Maybe it's the beginnings of hunger and thirst from the fasting, or maybe it's the thought of watching Darren and Isabelle eat and flirt with each other all through lunch. Whatever it is, the serene feeling from this morning has completely disappeared.

Lunchtime comes around way too quickly, and I'm dreading it. I take my time making my way to the lunch hall. The place is massive and overcrowded, so it takes me a while to find Isabelle and Darren sitting at one of the horizontal metal trestle tables.

It's as loud as ever, and my head pounds. The smell of boiled potatoes and baked beans makes my stomach turn. Darren sees me and waves me over, so I make my way towards them. As I get closer, Darren appears even more gorgeous. He is wearing smart black trousers and a black and white checked shirt. He looks so dapper, but it's that dreamy intense look he has that makes my breath catch. His hair is floppy today and he keeps pushing it out of his eyes. God, those eyes!

Get rid of those thoughts, Aisha, it's Ramadan; now is not the time.

"Hey, Aisha," he says with a huge smile. "You alright?"

I sit down and beads of sweat collect on my nose again. I grab a napkin from Isabelle's tray and wipe them off.

"Where's your lunch tray?" he asks.

"Oh, I'm not having lunch today."

"Why not?" Isabelle frowns.

"I'm fasting," I explain. "It's Ramadan."

"Oh, I'm so sorry, I forgot!" says Darren.

"You know about Ramadan?" I ask, surprised.

"All my mates from my old school used to do it. I better call them later and see how they're doing. I feel really bad now, I shouldn't be eating in front of you." He pushes his tray aside.

"It's fine," I say. I knew this would happen. People feel uncomfortable eating around others who are fasting, which is why I had wanted to avoid the canteen during Ramadan. "Go ahead, it really doesn't bother me."

"Well, you can have a drink, right?" Isabelle asks. "You can have my juice if you want."

"No, I'm not allowed water till sunset."

"What! And what time's sunset?"

"It's eight thirty this year."

"That's ridiculous! I think that's really wrong and unhealthy; you can't do that—go on have a drink." She holds out the carton to me.

"Isabelle." Darren gently pushes her arm down. "She's not allowed."

"It's kind of weird," Isabelle mumbles.

If she thinks fasting is weird, maybe she thinks I'm weird?

"So how do you like our school?" I ask Darren. "What do you think of it so far?"

"Yeah, it's alright. Everyone's really friendly."

Isabelle glances at Darren and gives him a goofy smile, which he seems to ignore.

"Darren, do you fancy going to the cinema this weekend?" she asks, giggling.

You can tell she's been building up to this moment for ages. I don't know why but I feel myself cringing on her behalf.

"What, all of us you mean? Depends what's on."

Isabelle shoots me a look and I respond straightaway, "You guys go ahead, I'll be fasting and stuff, so won't be able to make it."

Isabelle goes on her phone and lists all the films that are showing at the local cinema. "We could go see the horror movie or this other one that's a romcom, what do you reckon?"

Darren shifts uncomfortably in his seat. "None of that really appeals to me. Why don't we wait till after Ramadan? Then Aisha can come too."

Isabelle scowls at me.

"Oh no, seriously you guys go, I really don't mind. I'll come some other time."

Darren shakes his head. "Nah, leave it for now, none of these movies look any good."

Isabelle glowers at him.

"What sort of movies are you into, Aisha?" Darren asks.

"I like Marvel and superhero films," I say. "I loved the *Joker*, it was amazing. But to be honest, I like all those superhero TV shows you know, like *Daredevil* and *Jessica Jones*. Oh, and I love *Cobra Kai*."

Darren seems impressed. "That's some violent stuff."

"Well, I have brothers so what do you expect?" I laugh.

We're smiling at each other and Isabelle's frowning at us. I instantly stop laughing. She stands abruptly, and Darren and I stare at her.

"I'm going to get some dessert." She puts a hand on Darren's shoulder. "Are you coming, babe?"

Babe?! She's calling him babe already!

Darren frowns at her, then shakes his head. Isabelle's mouth goes tight before she walks away.

CHAPTER EIGHT

Now it's just the two of us, I'm growing uncomfortable. "I might go too," I say. "I've got some stuff I need to finish."

"Oh, do you have to go?"

He looks genuinely disappointed. It's on the tip of my tongue to ask, and I try to ignore it, but I can't. "Why did you want me here at lunch?"

He shrugs. "Isabelle insisted we have lunch today. I only came along because she said you'd be coming."

"Really?" My thoughts are spinning, and I feel queasy. "But aren't you two . . ." I swallow hard, ". . . together?"

Darren laughs. "No! What gave you that idea? We're just mates. I'm not with anyone."

We hold each other's gaze, and it feels like we're the only people in the room, then Darren coughs, breaking the contact.

"I'm really sorry that I forgot about Ramadan."

"Don't worry about it. Were there lots of Muslims in your old school?"

If only there was one other Muslim here, I would feel I had an ally.

"I went to school in Bow, it was ninety-eight percent

Muslims. I know loads of Bangladeshi swear words; I can teach you if you like." He laughs.

I smile. "Maybe when Ramadan is over you can? Why did you move?"

"My mum died last year." His jaw tenses. "My dad got a promotion here and he said we needed the extra money. Plus, my grandma lives nearby, and she's got dementia, so he said we have to look after her. By which he means *I* have to look after her."

"Oh, my God, that sounds so tough."

As annoying as mine is, I don't know what I'd do without my mum.

"It's not a whole lot of fun, to be honest."

"I'm sorry," I say. "That's a lot of responsibilities to deal with. I can't imagine how hard it is."

He furrows his brow. "Don't get me wrong, Aisha, I love my grandmother, I really do, but yeah, I sometimes wish I didn't have to deal with it."

"Can't you get a carer for her or something?"

"We've got some who come in for a few hours," Darren says, pushing his food around his tray. "But my dad won't pay for more. He says he's not frittering away his hard-earned cash when I'm around to help. 'Man up, and stop being such a Zoomer,' he keeps telling me. God, I hate that expression. It's like you can't ever admit that anything bothers you, otherwise you're weak and not a real man. You know he even told me to man up when we left the church after burying my mum."

Wow, this poor guy. I want to comfort him and say some-thing to make him feel better, but then Isabelle comes back.

"Why so serious you two? What are you talking about?"

"Oh, nothing." Darren shoots me a look as if to tell me not to say anything.

"I've really got to go." I stand to leave.

"Stay," Darren says. But Isabelle gives me a look and it's clear she wants Darren all to herself.

"I'll hang out longer next time," I promise as I gather my things and leave the table.

By the time I get home from school I have a splitting headache. I think it's the lack of water. I take Mum's advice and sleep for a bit. When I wake, my lips are parched and almost stuck together. I get up and rinse out my mouth. It's six thirty pm, another two hours to go. I try to remember what Shafqat Aunty told me about how I'm doing this for Allah, and it's not meant to be easy.

I keep busy, it's the only way to make the time go quicker. Mum and I pray together and then I help her prepare the Iftar which we will eat when we break the fast. I chop and slice and stir and fry, and it helps pass the time. Apart from the challenge of thirst and hunger, I must keep fighting the images of Darren from my mind. I keep thinking about the cinema, picturing me and him there instead of him and Isabelle. We wouldn't be watching some trashy B-rate horror movie though; it would be a proper romance like *The Kissing Booth* or *After* or something.

Stop it, Aisha. I cannot think about him right now so why does he keep popping into my brain?

Towards the end of the fast, the simplest of movements is

making me tired. The minutes counting down to eight thirty seem like the longest moments of my life. Mum and Dad are snappy with each other.

"There's no point fasting if you cannot keep your temper," Mum says to him.

"What would you know? You don't have to work all day and fast. You just stay home and do nothing," Dad retorts.

I can feel a fight about to break out so I quietly say, "Let's discuss this after Iftar, shall we?"

No one responds, but Mum glares at Dad.

So much for fasting teaching self-control.

There are only five minutes left and Burhan's watching cartoons on the TV.

"Change it to the Islam channel, Burhan," Mum says.

He chooses to ignore her as usual.

Dad snaps, "Change it now or you will be in big trouble."

I think for a moment about the type of trouble I would be in if Mum and Dad knew all the thoughts that I'd been having all day.

Burhan sighs and rolls his eyes but changes the channel. There's an advert on for a Halal steak place, the images of sizzling meat are almost too much to bear. I shut my eyes briefly. I don't want to see.

We sit around the table and start filling our plates. Mum has already placed a juicy Palestinian date on each plate. I try not to think about the dream where Darren placed the date in my mouth—this so isn't the time or place. I take one samosa and one pakora and place a dollop of Mum's amazing green coriander chutney next to the samosa ready to dip, any minute now. Mum spoons onto her plate a ladleful of the black chana she's been busy preparing in her massive pressure cooker, then Dad places some of the special raw lentil salad he has made with crushed chilli and garlic pieces on top. I take some salad and some fruit salad. My plate is practically overflowing.

There's a massive jug of Jam-e-shirin in the middle of the table, the bright pink drink they make every year. It's like rose water with cubes of ice and lemon, and tons of sugar in it. I can't stand it, it's so sickly sweet, so when Mum tries to pour it into my glass, I shake my head and she glares at me a little.

"It is good for dehydration, you know," she says.

"I don't like it." I grab the apple juice and pour that into my glass instead.

The adverts are nearly over, and they've started the dua, the prayer, but it's still not time to eat. I try to focus on the prayer.

"Oh, Allah, I have fasted for You, I believe in You, and I put my trust in You, and I break my fast with Your sustenance. The thirst has gone, and the veins are quenched, and reward is confirmed if Allah wills."

I try to think about what these words mean, and I'm suddenly overcome by a feeling of pride about the sacrifice I've made today for the sake of my belief. Shafqat Aunty was right, surely Allah would help me find peace.

Finally, the image on the television changes to one of the Kaaba and the people pouring in and out. The relief of finally hearing the Adhan, the call to prayer, on the Islam channel is indescribable.

As I place the juicy brown date in my mouth, a great sense of wellbeing comes over me. I drink slowly and eat slowly, but within a few mouthfuls I'm full, happy, and slightly drowsy. We do our prayers and I feel a lot better. I stuff Mum's rotis down way too fast and then my tummy starts to hurt.

"Aisha, you should eat slowly; now you will have gas. Go lay down otherwise you will be sick," Mum says.

I lay on my bed and listen to 'To Be So Lonely' by Harry Styles. My thoughts immediately go to Darren. I feel so bad for him stuck at home with only his grandmother for company. I wonder if he gets lonely. Does he like me? Or does he like Isabelle? Maybe, I'm crazy, but for all Isabelle's flirting, I can't help thinking it's me he likes and not her.

The song switches to 'Golden' and for some reason it makes me think of his eyes. Those eyes, I could just drown in them, they seem to take me to another world. His smile is amazing, but best is the fact that he seems to get me. He's so nice. He saved me from those bullies, asked for my number, he doesn't fancy Isabelle, and he actually knows about Ramadan. The way he looks at me is as if it's only me and him in the whole wide world. I'm out of breath just thinking about it.

Is there any point denying it? I'm so into him. I can't stop thinking about him ALL THE TIME. I've never felt like this before. Could this be love? Maybe he's The One?

I want to laugh and cry at the same time. It's like I've been given this amazing gift, but at the same time I'm so scared because I know nothing can happen between us. A great hole opens in my chest through which I think I might sink and disappear never to be seen again. What a time and what a choice—falling in love with a white boy during Ramadan. It's hopeless, worse than hopeless. My family would be furious.

My community would disown me. Shafqat Aunty would be so disappointed. I might be sent away to Pakistan. It's all so frightening.

My eyes well up with bitter tears. I know there's no way I can ever be with him, but I want him so bad it hurts.

Despite my fasting, I find no peace. I haven't learned self-control at all. All I have is nausea and emptiness, and a great weight on my chest, but then like a light in the darkness, an idea starts to take shape. I sit upright. What if Darren became a Muslim? He knows so much about the Muslim faith, he said most of his old friends were Muslim. . . maybe he would. . . maybe he could. . . maybe I could get him to convert?

Yes, Darren can convert! I know it sounds mad, but what if it worked? Surely, I must have met him for a reason? Allah wouldn't have put him in my path just to torment me. No, this is destiny. If he's Muslim, my family would be more accepting of him and then we could date, maybe even get married and have lots of gorgeous kids. My heart sings at the thought of it, but I need a plan to make him see the benefits of becoming a Muslim.

CHAPTER NINE

Now I've finally admitted to myself how I feel about Darren, it's like a huge weight's been lifted off me. I keep staring at Darren's Instagram profile picture, not daring to send him a friend request. Why doesn't he send me one? Maybe he's at home looking at my profile too? I've updated it to my prettiest picture where my skin looks perfect and I'm staring directly at the camera, just in case he does look me up.

I feel like one of those drug addicts you see in films that do nothing but think about drugs, and the less they have them, the more they want them, until they go crazy. It's like my brain doesn't belong to me anymore: only thoughts of Darren are allowed. Why is it the more you can't have something, the more you want it? I want to tell him how I feel, but I can't—he has to be a Muslim first. Until then, what do I do with all these feelings? I've never felt like this before: out of breath, and my stomach almost hurting from all the butterflies. How do I act *normal* around him? I have no idea. So, I do the only sensible thing—I ignore him.

It's hard to avoid someone when you're in the same classes. I try to get there early and nab a seat with someone else before he has any chance of sitting with me. I avoid all eye contact, even though I pass him constantly in the hallway.

Once Ramadan is over, I figure I'll work on my plan then. The main problem is, how am I going to persuade him to convert? Everywhere you look, Muslims have a bad name. If you switch on the news and hear the word Muslim, you can bet it will be followed by a picture of a bomb or the word *radicalisation,* or an image of a hijabi with a Kalashnikov. I remember watching a TV cop show about a Muslim girl from Bosnia, and the cops even talked about the stereotypes of Muslim terrorists, but then right at the end she blows up a building anyway!

Sometimes I feel like screaming, "We're not all like that you know! We're not all terrorists and bombers!" But I wonder if anyone would believe me. I mean there are bad people from all religions but why is it only Muslims that have the bad rep? Bad people are just bad people.

Mum's friend Shelley is Irish, and I remember her saying that in the eighties when she worked in the city, whenever she answered the phone, her Irish accent would scare people. They all assumed she was part of the IRA! She laughs about it now, but she says it hurt at the time.

The thing that really scares me is that even little kids seem to be saying nasty things. Burhan was saying the other day that when some kid found out he was Muslim, he laughed and said, "When you walk into the room, the room goes boom!" He tried to laugh it off, but I could tell he was upset. When Dad suggested we complain, he just said, "No way! I'm no snitch."

But not everyone's like that. Darren's not. He's tolerant and understanding and sees beyond the hate. The other problem is Isabelle. How can I justify trampling all over her feelings and going for the boy she likes? We've been friends since we were eleven, back when we bonded over how weird the geography teacher was. We were so mad back then. I remember I had a tennis ball, and we named it Leslie and pretended it was a dog. I used to make Isabelle pet it and kiss it, and she would do it too. We even sent each other Christmas cards from Leslie. We hung out practically every day after school at her massive house. She was so sweet back then, but lately she's changed. Since she got her braces removed and learned how to do make up and wear her hair down, it's like she's realised that she's actually pretty. And now she's into boys, that's kind of all she ever talks about.

But she does have a good sense of when I feel like I'm missing out, and she does make an effort to include me. Like the other day, including me in lunch when I was all alone. When I think about that it makes me feel bad. I know that Darren doesn't belong to anyone, and he said they were just friends, but she clearly likes him.

Do I just ignore that I like him, and that he seems to like me back?

It's all too complicated.

Towards the end of Ramadan, it's a particularly hot day, and the fasting's really getting to me. I'm hot and thirsty and weak, and it seems like the days are dragging on forever. I'm standing by my locker and struggling to think what books I'm meant to be taking out—is it chemistry or maths next? Everything is just a big blur. Then I feel a tap on my shoulder.

I turn around to find Darren leaning with one hand pressed against my locker. I'm practically rammed against it and there's hardly any space between us. The smell of his deodorant is overpowering.

"Are you avoiding me?"

I stand there with my parched lips moving silently, trying to think of what to say in response. Why is his face so blurry? My head is spinning. What should I say? God, why can't I think of something to say?

"Darren, I . . ."

But the heat is too much and before I know it, everything goes black.

When I wake, Darren and a couple of his mates from football club—I think they're called Luke and Sam—are gathered around staring at me, asking if I'm okay. I struggle to focus. I try to sit up, but everything is spinning. Someone pushes me gently back down, which is probably for the best.

"How long was I out for?" I ask Darren.

"I don't know, maybe thirty seconds," Darren says, his face crinkled up with worry.

The school nurse is called, a middle-aged Irish woman with short hair and a concerned face, and I get carted off to her office. Darren comes with me and tells the nurse that I've been fasting. I'm forced to eat a stale custard cream and drink some orange juice.

I feel horrible eating; it seems so wrong to break my fast, but what choice do I have?

The nurse calls my parents to come and collect me, so

Darren waits with me. I'm sitting in a plastic chair facing the window, and he's leaning against the shelf near the sink. He pulls up another chair and puts his hands in mine. They're warm and soft.

"I'm sorry you had to break your fast. I feel bad, I guess it's like when we have Lent and aren't allowed to eat certain things."

Oh, he's a Christian. "Yeah, well, it's not your fault."

"I feel like it is. Sorry if I came at you aggressively. I just wanted to know why you've stopped talking to me."

I look up at his concerned face. He's really bothered that I've been ignoring him. So, I am on his radar after all.

"I've just been busy fasting and studying and stuff. Why do you care anyway?"

His face crumples as if I've slapped him or something. I hadn't meant it in a nasty way.

He glances around the office to check we're alone. "I think you know why. I like you, Aisha, I really like you."

CHAPTER TEN

I look at the floor, at my hands, my shoes—anywhere but him. My chest physically hurts as though my ribs are going to break. I wish I could just say, *of course I know why, and I feel the same way,* but I can't. He's not a Muslim. All we can do is walk around all the stuff we want to say to each other.

The door opens, and the nurse comes in.

"Your mum is here now, Aisha. You go on home and take some rest. You'll be bright as a button by the morning."

"Thank you." I stand, feeling less lightheaded. Darren has his arm out as if ready to catch me if I fall. "Thank you so much for waiting and looking after me when I fainted."

He doesn't say anything, just looks at me with those eyes and gives me the briefest of nods.

I wish I could say how much I care, but I can't. I blink quickly trying to stop myself from bursting into tears.

When I get home, Mum points at the stairs.

"You go to your bed and no fasting tomorrow, you understand me?"

Mum looks at me in a way that says she doesn't want to hear any complaints, so I go upstairs and lay on my bed. I don't want to sleep. I'm full of energy having eaten during the day, and I've got Darren to think about.

In my mind, I replay over and over when he said *I really like you, Aisha.* I think back to the way it felt when he leaned towards me before I blacked out. He was so close, his lips so near to mine, and the smell of him was intoxicating. For a moment, I shut my eyes and imagine him leaning forward those extra few inches and kissing me. I snap them open again and try to remove the image.

Stop kidding yourself Aisha, I tell myself. Sure, maybe he's interested, but he's off limits. There's no way he'd convert for you. He might fancy you, but that doesn't mean he's in love with you. Not enough to convert, that's for sure.

I play Taylor's swift 'Style' in the background. Then I look in the mirror. Without my hijab, my hair hangs down past my shoulders and it's thick and glossy. I have large brown eyes, which several people commented on at the gathering I went to with Shafqat Aunty. Then there's my figure. I've never really looked at my body closely before, but suddenly, I'm overwhelmed by the desire to look at myself and see how much I've changed.

I go to my door and turn the lock. I close the curtains, strip down to my underwear, and stare at my reflection in the mirror. I've slimmed down with the fasting, and my stomach is flat and taut. My waist curves inward and then out again with my slim hips, giving me an hourglass figure, with breasts that seem larger than normal, maybe because my middle section is slimmer. I run my hand along my hips which feel smooth and soft. I can feel my breathing speeding up. I push my breasts together and I don't recognise the sexy girl peering back at me.

Still breathing heavily, I rush over to my underwear drawer and look for something more alluring than the tattered white knickers and bra that I'm wearing. The contents of my drawer doesn't resemble anything remotely sexy, only grey knickers and more off-white bras. Everything's so chaste. Why don't I own anything nice?

At the bottom of the drawer, I find my old black swimming costume. It's an all-in-one, and there are no holes or sections cut out or anything, but it's the sexiest item I have. I undress completely and tug it on. I go back to the mirror, pulling up my hair so that only the front sections are falling forward, and I have to say I look amazing. If only Darren could see me like this. I turn to the side and the contours of my bottom and legs look so enticing. Maybe I should take a selfie and send it to him. I know it's what loads of girls in my year do, but I can't. What if someone found it?

My muscles are tense, and I can feel a strange sensation pulling at my insides, something is happening to my body. I lay on my bed in my swimming costume, face forward, and the strange sensation seems to grow within me. I don't know if it's because I'm wearing the swimming costume, but I shut my eyes and imagine that I'm on the beach with Darren, facing him sideways, wearing these clothes and looking like this. I imagine him kissing me, his mouth on mine, his hand in my hair, waves crashing down on us, and I roll around in my bed . . .

A knock on the door makes me jump.

"Aisha, you are okay?" Mum asks.

I jump up and quickly pull on my dressing gown before I unlock the door.

"Sab theek?" Mum repeats her previous question in Urdu as she scrunches up her eyes and peers around my room.

"Yeah, why?"

"We hear some banging noise, so I come to look."

I try to ignore the heat rising in my face and burning my ears.

"I didn't hear anything," I mutter. "Mum, I'd like to fast tomorrow."

"Aisha you are not well today—I thought we already talk about this."

I cross my arms. "I don't care. I'm doing it. If you won't wake me up, I'll just set an alarm on my phone."

"Your wish." She leaves, shaking her head and mumbling something under her breath about teenagers.

After she's gone, I take off the dressing gown and swimming costume, and change into my fluffy pink pyjamas. I stare at the crumpled swimming costume on the floor. I feel disgusted with myself. These thoughts I'm having are wrong. It is un-Islamic to be dreaming and thinking of a non-Muslim boy like this. I must fight the *nafs,* my desires. I must fast; I must purge myself of these sins.

CHAPTER ELEVEN

Ramadan is finally over. I don't want to admit it, but I'm relieved. I found it hard, and I'm looking forward to not feeling thirsty and tired all the time. My body has grown used to the lack of food in the daytime so I'm not even hungry anymore. Eid falls on a Wednesday, and luckily the school have agreed that I can take the day off.

I wake in the morning, excited and happy. It's still early because we have to get to the mosque on time. Mum has been awake for at least an hour, sorting out breakfast and special Eid snacks.

"Aisha, go and have your shower," Mum shouts up the stairs.

For me, this shower feels so special. I know that when I return to get changed, Mum will have laid out my new Eid clothes. Sure enough, there they are, together with brand new underwear. Mum always leaves the labels on, so we know for sure they've just been bought, but I'm horrified when I see my new clothes. It's a super-glitzy salwar kameez, white with silver embellishments all over the front, silver trim all along the floaty skirt section, and embroidered sequins all around the waist which glisten and sparkle dazzlingly. It's a beautiful outfit but it looks like something you might wear to a wedding, not to the mosque, especially as we have to walk there! What if we pass Darren at the bus stop? What on earth would he think of me?

"Mum, can you come upstairs?"

I hear her footsteps. "What is the problem?"

"I can't wear this," I say. "It's so over the top."

"Ya Khuda! When we were young, we used to wear nice clothes on Eid."

"Yes, but it's not meant to be a fashion show," I protest.

I'm especially annoyed as Mum's dressed in a dowdy brown salwar kameez.

"Young people today, all so boring," she complains. "I told you to come with me to choose the clothes, but you are too lazy and say you don't want to waste your whole day on the Green Street."

"Yeah, but that was because you said after Green Street we had to go and visit all your friends—I can't spend my whole day doing that!"

Mum is just as animated when she responds, "Well you should not complain that you don't like the kapre when you can't even be bothered to come and get them!" There's a tense pause. "Okay if you don't want to wear, I'll find something 'simple' for you. Never mind how much I spent on those clothes . . ."

"Okay, okay, I'll wear them," I say, the guilt heavy in my chest.

I don't want to fight on Eid, but I make a mental note-to-self to make sure I go shopping with her next year, instead of just leaving her to it. I put on the outfit. The white pleats hang down to the floor, and the shimmering silver waistband and bodice glisten in the mirror. Even the white hijab that came with it has sparkles all around the edges. Feeling ridiculous, I make my way downstairs.

My brothers and Dad sit around the breakfast table dressed up in their perfect white kurtas and with little caps on their heads. They smell lovely as they've already dabbed their wrists with ithar, a male perfume, like they always do on Eid. The ithar is in elegant bottles this year--Mum's Eid gift to Dad and the boys. The potent smell of sandalwood fills the air.

"See, you look lovely, beti," Mum says. "Doesn't Aisha look lovely?" Mum nudges Dad with her elbow.

"Yes, yes lovely," Dad mutters, more interested in wolfing down his breakfast.

The table looks magnificent. Mum has made shami kebabs, Dahi Bada, kheer and vermicelli covered with flaked almonds. I sit down excitedly and fill a little bowl with the kheer, the rice pudding which looks so yummy; I can't wait to try it. But after a month of fasting, what do you know, as soon as I eat a few spoonfuls, I feel like I'm going to explode.

"Mum, I can't eat any more," I complain.

"Just leave it then." She frowns and makes a face as though I'm always complaining.

"Anyway, we should go. We mustn't be late for the prayers," Dad says.

"Do we have to walk?" I ask, sweating. I really don't want anyone I know from school to see me, especially Darren.

"Of course we have to walk, we'll never get parked, you know that, Aisha. Why are you asking these silly questions?"

The awful boys from the other school are at the bus stop.

I see shaved head and skinny smirking at me, and I think there are some others. No Darren at least, thank goodness. He must have caught the earlier bus.

I stand out a mile in my glittering white costume. Then it starts: wolf whistling at first, and then shouting out abuse.

"The Pakis are out! Where you going? Off to bomb a building?"

Dad shoots them an angry glare and they just laugh.

"I told you we should have driven," I mutter.

"Ignore them, Aisha, they are ignorant people. I have been dealing with people like this all my life."

It's over in a flash but the jeering and shouting echo in my ears. My little brothers look like they are about to burst into tears. Burhan's lip quivers while Farhan, the youngest, asks me, "Why don't they like us?"

We stop walking for a minute. I bend down and cuddle him squeezing him tight, trying my best to comfort him even though I'm on the verge of tears myself. I don't want my brothers to see I'm just as upset as them.

"They're just not very smart."

"Someone at my school said halal meat is gross," Burhan says. "Maybe they think we're gross too."

Where are the kids at school getting these ideas from?

"Let us change the subject," Mum says. "Don't let these naughty people ruin your Eid."

We arrive at the mosque a few minutes later. It's a run-down old corner house with two separate entrances—one for men and the other for women. Mum and I split off from the boys and enter via the back. We're hit by the smell of shoe leather and sweaty feet. Everyone's taken off their shoes and placed them in the little box-shaped shoe-tidies by the entrance; I see an array of different styles from boring black flats to six-inch killer heels and I wonder who those belong to. We take our shoes off and place them in the plastic bag Mum has brought with her.

"Don't leave them here," Mum says. "We don't want them to get crushed like last year."

I nod. They were pretty damaged last time. She places them in her massive red handbag, and we make our way up the brown carpeted stairway to the women's prayer room. The same nasty, threadbare, dusty carpet is all over this room. They've placed a white sheet in some parts of the room, but it doesn't completely cover the carpet.

Mum dumps me pretty much immediately for her friends. I smile at a few ladies and sit down towards the front waiting for the prayers to start. While waiting in the mosque I can feel the other ladies staring at me disapprovingly. No one's dressed like me; they're all dressed down. I knew Mum didn't understand what people wore these days! Luckily, there is one other girl who seems really overdressed too—she must be the owner of the killer heels. I smile weakly at her, and she smiles back with a full mouth of red lipstick.

I don't really know these people; I literally only see them once a year. They come from all over, so even though there are some girls who look around the same age as me, I don't know who they are. I try to avoid eye contact and take my phone out of my handbag, hiding it from view so all the aunties don't start telling me off.

I switch it on and have loads of messages wishing me *Eid Mubarak*. Some of them are GIFs with images of fireworks and a new moon appearing. There's a funny meme from one of my cousins showing a man sitting in the mosque with his bum crack showing, saying 'The moon has been sighted, Eid Mubarak to all.' I suppress my laughter; the ladies wouldn't approve. When I scroll down though, I gasp.

No, I'm not imagining it.

DARREN: *Eid Mubarak, Aisha! Hope you have a lovely day, will miss you at school. D xx*

I want to grab the phone, hold it to my lips, and kiss the message on the screen. My face is hot, and I hope no one notices. Trust them to start calling for prayer now before I have time to read it again and again. Reluctantly I put my phone away.

When the prayer is over, I hug the other ladies, as is the custom and wish them all Eid Mubarak. They keep commenting how lovely and radiant I look. I don't know if they're being sarcastic and judging me, and to be honest, I don't really care. I don't even care about the boys at the bus stop. Darren remembered! That was all that mattered!

When we get back home, I rush to my bedroom—I want to look at the message again. What should I reply? *You're amazing and I love you!* Maybe that's too much. I reply, 'thank you' and at the last minute add a kiss.

CHAPTER TWELVE

On the way home from the mosque, I remember that everyone in there would disapprove if I dated Darren, but surely we're meant to be spreading Islam to new people. How am I going to convince him that becoming a Muslim is a good idea? I'm going to treat it like a homework assignment. I'll research online and then draw up a list with bullet points on how to achieve my goal, but it will have to be after the obligatory Eid lunch which this year happens to be massive.

Mum's been slaving away so I have to try and eat even though I really don't feel like it; things are tense enough because Dad's older sister Zarina Chachi has turned up. Mum hates her but has to pretend she likes her. I don't really blame her. Zarina Chachi can be quite bitchy to Mum. They're always competing over Dad's attention but she's really nice to me and my brothers though.

As soon as she arrives, Zarina Chachi hugs me. Our bony frames rub together painfully, and she thrusts twenty-five pounds into my hand.

"Eid Mubarak, darling Aisha," she says.

She does the same to my younger brothers who jump up

and down in delight, even though she squeezes their cheeks which they absolutely hate.

At lunchtime, Mum and I bring out a huge plate of biryani, a bowl of Indian vegetables, a meat dish, and a salad. It all smells amazing. Zarina Chachi doesn't offer to help and sits in her chair while Mum spoons food on to her plate. She takes a mouthful of rice and then makes a face.

"Rice is a bit sticky, isn't it?" she says.

Mum's face glowers, but she doesn't say anything. Her hand trembles, and I have a mental image of her smashing the spoon over Zarina Chachi's head.

I don't want to make Mum look bad by not eating much, but it's such an effort. My stomach has shrunk during Ramadan, and I can barely eat even though I'm hungry. I feel like one of those geese they breed to make *foie gras*. I've watched a documentary about it. They keep their mouths open with some horrible metal ring and then force feed them until their livers are three times the normal size. Okay so that's a bit dramatic, but why is there always so much emphasis on food?

"What's the matter, Aisha?" Zarina Chachi asks. "Why aren't you eating? You're not dieting, are you?"

I shake my head and shove more food into my mouth as Mum nods approvingly.

Zarina Chachi and Mum barely speak to each other, but Dad and the boys don't even seem to notice.

"I really enjoyed the talk at the mosque, Dad, didn't you?" I ask.

He nods. "Yes, very good, very good."

"Especially when he said there were two new people who had become Muslims."

"Ah yes, the converts," Mum says.

"Nowadays they call them reverts," I correct her. Mum and Zarina Chachi knit their brows. "Because they've reverted back to their original state of being born a Muslim."

Zarina Chachi rolls her eyes. "All these new-fangled things I don't understand. The only converts I know about are Muhammad Ali and Cat Stevens."

"Oh yeah, the boxer, right? That's so cool. Who's Cat Stevens?"

"You know, the singer? He changed his name to Yusuf Islam in the seventies," Dad explains. "And let us not forget Neil Armstrong."

"Oh, Dad, not all this again! How many times do I have to tell you that's a myth?"

When I was little, Dad told me a story about Neil Armstrong, the first man on the moon. Dad said that the reason he fluffed his lines 'one small step for man, one giant leap for mankind' instead of 'one small step for *a* man, one giant leap for mankind' was because when he landed on the moon, the first sound he heard was the adhan, the Muslim call to prayer. Apparently, he didn't recognise the sound at the time, but years later when he was in a Muslim country, he heard it again and realised what it was. He then apparently converted to Islam.

I was shocked when Dad told me. It totally proved to me the existence of Allah, so you can imagine my disappointment when I found a whole Wikipedia page proving that it was all a lie. Neil Armstrong even issued an official letter from the U.S. Department of State, insisting that any claims to conversion were inaccurate, yet Dad still believes it.

"Remember, I showed you that Wikipedia page and everything?" I say.

"I don't believe that." He shakes his head. "American propaganda."

I roll my eyes. Dad and his conspiracy theories. My stomach hurts, I'm so stuffed.

"I'm done, Mum, can I go upstairs?"

Mum waves her hand. I grin and stand up. I can tell that Zarina Chachi wants to say something, but I leave the table not giving her a chance. It's time to actually write this conversion plan.

I decide it will have to be divided into steps, that way I can ease Darren into it, but first I need to do some more research; I can't just rely on Dad's dodgy stories. Online I read the story about Cat Stevens, and of course, Muhammad Ali. Darren would have to be impressed by that one, right? Everyone loves Muhammad Ali. A lot of the stories have a common thread: the people were drifters with no sense of purpose. I read a story about some guy called Bilal who was born a Christian but became an atheist and then an agnostic. He was drawn in by the sense of community and strict discipline of Islam because it gave him a sense of belonging. I even read that Lindsay Lohan was reading the Qur'an and thinking of converting.

After three hours of online research, I have a plan.

Aisha's Ten Steps to helping Darren convert to Islam

1. Take Darren to the British Museum. He can see the Islamic Art section, then he will realise how much Muslims have contributed to history and culture. I

can say it's to help with our history homework, which it kind of is.

2. Take Darren to one of Shafqat Aunty's charity events and then he will see we're not all weird bombers and terrorists but kind people who want to help others. There's that fair coming up and they need volunteers. I'll tell him about the free pizza for people who help out—who doesn't like pizza? I bet all the aunties will go crazy for him, he's so handsome.

3. Take Darren to a mosque—a really cool one, like that Regent's Park Mosque with the golden dome. Imagine how beautiful it would be glistening in the sunlight.

4. Introduce him to some converts/reverts —that will defo inspire him.

I feel like by step 4 he will be so interested, I can start teaching him a bit about what being a Muslim is.

5. Try to get Darren to read some of the Qur'an. It's not so different to the Bible, a lot of the stories are almost the same. Maybe I could slip a leaflet into his locker or even the translation of that beautiful passage *Ayat Al-Kursi*? Darren said he had gone to church when his mum died so I'm sure he's a Christian.

6. Get Darren to see there's not much difference between Islam and Christianity. All he has to realise is that we believe Jesus is not God, he's a prophet.

7. Tell him about the Day of Judgement which is not so different from in the Bible: we will be holding hands at the gates of heaven for ever and ever.

8. Tell Darren that we are all born Muslims so it won't be a big deal converting, he will just be going back to his natural state.

9. Tell him about Fate, that God has ordained all things—nothing occurs without his will. It's clear that we're drawn together for a purpose, which means we HAVE to be together.

Once he has completed steps 5 to 9, he will agree to revert, and I can imagine his beautiful lips mouthing the Shahada.

10. *'La illaha ill allah, Muhammadur Rasullulla'* which means 'I testify that there is no other God but Allah, and Muhammad is God's messenger.'

Then he will be committed to being a Muslim.

I'm pretty impressed by my plan, but then it occurs to me that I've drawn all these comparisons with Christianity to make him feel it wasn't such a big step, but I don't really know how religious he is. I groan. Is this a stupid plan? But then as clear as day, I hear Shafqat Aunty's voice in my ear, *'Allah will find a way.'*

CHAPTER THIRTEEN

It's one thing writing the list, but another thing putting it into action. How am I supposed to present this to Darren without him thinking it's weird? I've printed out the list, folded it up, and put it in my jacket pocket, but as I walk through the school gates, it hits me how ridiculous this plan is—is love actually making me crazy?

I walk through the school hall. It's bustling as usual, kids rushing to classes and trying to grab books from their lockers.

"I was so pissed this weekend, that party was epic," Luke with the scruffy brown hair and just a hint of a moustache says. Sam, a curly blonde-haired boy, slams his locker shut and Luke winces, holding the side of his head. "Don't bang the locker, it's doing my head in, fam."

They're Darren's mates from football. I wonder what they would think if they saw my list.

I stand at the side feeling left out; all this talk of alcohol and parties that I miss out on. I just want to get to my locker and get my books out. Where is Darren? At this rate I'm not going to see him till the afternoon when we have chemistry together. Morning is double maths which means two hours of Isabelle. What if she finds out about my plan?

As soon as I enter the classroom and sit at my desk, Isabelle is hounding me. "Where were you yesterday?"

"I told you, it was Eid. You know, the end of Ramadan, big celebrations, food and more food."

"Oh, that's why you have a pot belly today." She laughs. "Only joking."

My hands go straight to my stomach. I do feel a bit bloated, but I don't really see how as I barely ate anything, but now I feel self-conscious and stretch out my T-shirt with my hands so it's not clinging to me.

"Anyway, guess what happened? I asked Darren out again yesterday and he said he would think about it!"

I feel like the room is spinning. My ears burn and I feel dizzy. I've just drawn up this list—my whole ten-point plan! What is she talking about?

"What do you mean? Last time you said you thought he wasn't that into you."

Isabelle frowns. "I don't remember saying that. We've been having lunch together. I think cos you were fasting you haven't been around much. We've got really close."

I suppose I had been in a daze the whole month, a blissful, half-starved, kidding-myself naive daze. So the entire time I was fasting and praying, the whole world was passing me by. There I was dreaming about Darren, completely oblivious to the fact that he was interested in my friend the whole time. But why did he tell me he liked me when I fainted at school? Then I remember what Shafqat Aunty would say, that this must be the latest of Shaitan's attempts to lead me astray.

Waves of nausea sweep through my stomach and my face feels like it's on fire.

"I've told him the plan is to go to the cinema and then to dinner. I'm totally going to pick something romantic to watch."

Her grin is so annoying. The smug look makes me want to punch her! Worried that my face is showing what I'm thinking, I force myself to smile.

"Will you two girls stop gossiping!" Miss Evans says, peering over her glasses. "You're not in year seven anymore, can you focus on your work? I would have thought a girl like you, Aisha, would be interested in doing well in your A-levels, instead of chatting all the time."

What was that supposed to mean? *A girl like me.*

I'm silent the rest of the maths lesson pretending to focus on my work. My head's pounding and I can almost hear the blood flowing through my ears.

Why is Darren leading me on? What is he playing at? One minute he's telling me he likes me, the next he's thinking of going out with Isabelle. What the hell?

Isabelle has her saxophone lesson at lunchtime. I'm relieved that I don't have to hear about Darren but eating alone sucks. I'm sitting with my miserable cheese sandwich on my pathetic little lunch tray, at the back of the lunch hall. The stink of boiled cabbage that's a permanent smell in the canteen, doesn't seem to have got any better since Ramadan finished. The metal table feels sticky and greasy under my fingers.

A tray lands on the table in front of me.

"Mind if I sit here?" Darren asks, not waiting for me to respond as he pulls out a chair.

I always think I'm going to be cool around him but

whenever we're together, the butterflies in my stomach are so crazy, I feel like I might explode.

"How was Eid?" he asks.

I can't believe it; he's already thinking about Islam! This is going to be easy.

"Good and thanks for checking in."

Is it my imagination or are groups of kids on other tables staring at us? There seems to be a lull in the noise levels in the dining hall.

"How have you been? Isabelle said you're going on a date this weekend."

He looks taken aback, his eyes widen, and then he laughs out loud. "I'm not going on a date with Isabelle. I only said I would think about it to get her off my case, she just kept asking and asking, and I didn't want to offend her. Wait, are you jealous, Aisha?" he asks slowly, as if he can't quite believe that I'm capable of envy.

"Maybe," I say, surprising myself with my honesty.

"Wow! You're not holding back today, are you? I was going to text her later to say I was busy."

I breathe a sigh of relief. They're not going out and he doesn't fancy her.

"Do you want me to take you on a date instead?" He's leaning forward now, those eyes seeing right through me, trying to figure out what's going on in my mind.

Yes, I do, I so want him to take me on a date. But I can't say that.

"Well, not a date exactly," I mumble. This is it, time to implement step one of the plan. "I want you to help me with our history homework."

"What?" He shakes his head and leans backwards in his chair. "The history homework is about Islam. You should be helping me!"

"Well, not help help. I just mean I want us to do it together. . . what do you think?"

"Okay, it will be fun to hang out."

I can't believe he went for it; he must really like me. The feeling of empowerment makes me bold.

"I need to ask you something else," I say.

"Yeah?"

"What religion are you?"

He stares at me, a line appearing between his eyebrows. "Wow, that's a bit random. I grew up Christian but I dunno. I don't really know what to believe since my mum died. Why are you asking?"

"No reason," I say quickly.

This might not be as easy as I thought.

"So, Saturday for our non-date?" he asks.

I laugh. "Yeah, I was thinking we could go to the British Museum. The essay is about the rise of the Islamic Empire, and they have loads of displays and stuff there." I'm holding my breath and praying that he'll buy it as I'm saying this.

"The British Museum?" Darren looks completely unenthused. "That's pretty far. It'll be so boring. Let's just go to the library and get it over and done with. Maybe after we could grab a coffee or something."

"Oh, go on, the tour is meant to be amazing," I plead. I bat my eyelashes at him the way I've seen Isabelle do with so many boys, and she always gets what she wants.

"If it means so much to you then sure, we can go there. Anything for you."

Waves of electricity seem to flow through me. Anything for me?

CHAPTER FOURTEEN

After lunch, Darren and I are partnered up in chemistry and we're doing a practical on equilibrium. I pour in colourless solution X and he pours in colourless solution Y, and when it mixes it turns brilliant orange, fizzing and bubbling. There's this moment when our fingers touch—that fizz feels more intense and electric than the fizz produced by the combined solutions. The brilliant orange almost sums up our relationship. Without each other, our lives are dull and colourless but if we could be together, we could be so much more. But there comes a saturation point, where it stops working. That must be where Isabelle comes in. If only I could get rid of that nagging guilty feeling at the back of my mind all the time.

I don't see Isabelle the rest of the day, but when I get home I receive a text from her.

ISABELLE: *Darren's such a jerk, he's told me we can't go out this weekend after all. Please don't tell anyone I even asked him out. X*

Bad doesn't begin to describe how I feel, but it's not as though he likes her. Am I breaking girl code? Does it count if the feelings are not mutual? Even if I wasn't in the picture, he was never going to take her out anyway. My head is pounding, and I massage my temples. All these emotions are giving me a headache.

If I thought overcoming the guilt would be easy, I was sorely mistaken. Isabelle keeps texting me saying she doesn't know what his problem is, and I don't know what to reply. On Saturday, before Darren and I are due to meet, she texts me again.

ISABELLE: *You seriously need to see his Instagram, it's so weird. Check out his mates.*

ME: *I'm not his friend on Instagram and I think his account is private.*

ISABELLE: *Look this is how much of a friend I am to you—use my login details and take a look. But you have to promise to delete my details after.*

She sends me her login. I go on my phone and am finally able to access his account. This is so exciting! I'm already familiar with his gorgeous profile picture. I click on his story but it's some boring meme about some footballers I've never heard of. He has a few posts but not many, mainly posts about tennis, Wimbledon, the French open. But there are also a lot of posts about some human rights campaigns he's part of like freeing Nazanin Zaghari-Ratcliffe. I love that he cares about this stuff.

I scroll through and see a list of girls—Faiza, Aalia, Sumayah, Sabiha, Humaira, the list goes on and on. I stare at the screen more closely. There are too many female friends. Young, pretty, Asian girls, some with hijabs and lots of makeup with massive eyelashes.

ME: *I've checked it out—what are you freaking out about? All the girls with headscarves?*

ISABELLE: *Yh*

ME: *He's from Bow, loads of girls wear headscarves there.*

ISABELLE: *But not a lot of male friends—it's weird. A bit creepy, don't you think?*

Up until yesterday Isabelle thought he was gorgeous, funny how she's changed her tune since he's gone off her. Creepy? Really? I roll my eyes. But not even I can ignore that he follows a lot of Asian girls. I shake my head. I'm not going to let it ruin our trip to the museum, so I delete Isabelle's login details and vow not to snoop on his Instagram profile again.

I've nicked Mum's concealer from her room, and I apply it over the tiny dark patches on my cheeks. I put on red lipstick but it's too loud, so I wipe it off. My outfit is simple— black jeans, a pink top with a light-coloured jacket, and my trademark black hijab. The list of Ten Steps is tucked in the inside pocket of my jacket. I've told Mum and Dad that the school has insisted I go to the British Museum for an assignment, and they seem to buy it.

CHAPTER FIFTEEN

"Hey, Aisha." Darren waves from outside the station. "You look different. Are you wearing makeup?"

Oh my God, he noticed!

"Just a bit." I blush.

"You look really nice. Shall we go?" He holds his arm out and I link onto it, a warm feeling filling my body.

We take a train first, and then a tube to the British Museum. We have such a laugh; Darren tells me all about how awkward it is in history because he has to sit next to this rugby player called Jason who picks his nose all the time.

"It's like so gross." He laughs. "I swear he eats it sometimes."

"Eurgh!" I grimace.

"You're like a hick from Hicksville," Darren teases when he sees me staring at the tube map like it's written in a foreign language. He understands it so well and works out all the changes easily.

Because it's so busy on the tube, there are times when we end up squashed against each other. We can't help exchanging glances that make me feel all tingly.

"Check out that Asian dude with the blue hair," he whispers to me. We're standing in the middle of the tube, clinging on to the central red pole and facing each other. He's so close, and smiling, and I can't help smiling back.

"Where?"

"Behind you." I start to turn, and he laughs. "Don't make it so obvious."

"Okay, chill." I manoeuvre myself so I can see. The man's shocking blue hair really doesn't go with his business suit.

"You are so mean." I giggle. "He's cool, he's probably into K-pop or something."

"Then why are you pissing yourself laughing?"

It's true, I can't stop giggling and I have to put my hand over my mouth. A strand of my hair comes loose and brushes against my cheek, and Darren leans forward and tucks it back under my hijab. As his fingers touch my skin, I feel pulses of electricity. We lock eyes and I catch my breath. His gaze slowly travels across my face which I can feel turning red, so I quickly turn away.

The tube is so hot that by the time we get out, my armpits feel clammy. God, I hope I haven't got huge sweat patches! When we step outside Russell Square station, it's buzzing. London is full of life and movement wherever you look. There are flash cars zooming past and the tall buildings look so grand. I smell food too, maybe pizza from one of the many cafés. The sun is out, and it feels gorgeous on my skin. We cross a huge green square, and I look up at the trees that are so vibrant it feels like we've stepped into a painting.

Darren stares at me for a moment, his eyes glistening in the sunlight. "Are you sure we can't just hang out here for the rest of the day?"

This isn't part of the plan! Although it's tempting to sit

around on this beautiful lawn and have a whole day together in the sun, I must stay focused. The temptation to ditch the plan is strong, especially when I see all the kids with ice creams, and couples on picnic blankets.

I laugh. "I'm already tanned, I don't need to sunbathe. Plus, we really have to get this homework done."

"Alright then, miss Try Hard. Whatever makes you happy."

Is that what he thinks of me? That I'm just a boring geek?

"Aisha, I'm kidding," he says as if he hears my thoughts. "I love that you're so into this."

I smile, relieved. "Okay, good." I hope he gets into it too.

The front of the museum is majestic. The huge columns framing the main entrance are visible through the black iron gates and make the building look like a gigantic Greek temple. Not really what you expect to see in the middle of a city.

"Isn't it cool?" I gush.

"Totally cool." He laughs. "You know what, those columns kind of remind me of Ripple chocolate bars. God I'm hungry."

My heart sinks. I'm not sure he's into this. Maybe once he gets inside and sees all the beautiful Islamic pieces, things will change.

"Do you want to get a coffee and cake?" I suggest. "I think there's a café inside."

"Sure, I'd love to have a coffee with you."

Maybe we can just stay in the café gazing into each other's eyes? No, Aisha! Focus!

"We have to be quick because the tour starts in forty-five minutes."

"Which tour is it again?" he asks. He's standing so close

to me that every time his arm brushes mine, it makes my skin feel like it's on fire.

"The... err... guided Islamic tour that will help us with our homework," I manage. "The one I've been telling you about."

"Oh, right, yeah."

"It's meant to be amazing."

"It sounds cool. We'll do the tour, but we need cake and coffee first."

When we enter the building, I gasp. I've never been here before and it's breathtaking. The ground floor is massive, and the sunrays that filter through the tessellated glass ceiling bounce off the white marble, making the whole space feel surreal. I feel like I've seen it before, and I'm trying to place where.

"Darren." I tug at his sleeve. "This place was in a movie."

"What movie?"

"This Indian movie Mum loves, *Kal Ho Naa Ho*." I glance at him.

"Kal what?"

"It means 'we don't know if there will be a tomorrow or not'," I explain, feeling self-conscious because my language must sound so strange to him.

"Any good?"

I nod. I don't tell him it's a love story that made me and Mum bawl our eyes out. Maybe it's a sign that this is a place for romance.

"This place is pretty cool," he says.

Yes! He's getting into it; the plan is falling into place.

"Okay, cake and coffee time," I say.

I order a latte, and Darren gets a coffee and a cake from

the ridiculously overpriced café on the ground floor. He offers to pay for my latte, which isn't only sweet, but comes as a relief, as paying for that alone would have been half my weekly allowance. We sit on a trestle table without much space to move around. I can't say I mind—it gives me an excuse to get close to him.

"So, this is the place with the mummies, right?" he says, glancing around. "We should so go to that bit. Did you know they used to suck out their brains through their eye sockets when they died?"

"Maybe we can look at that bit after," I suggest. "But we really ought to go on that tour."

"Don't worry, babe, we'll go." He ever so gently strokes my little finger. I love that he called me babe.

The tour is set to start somewhere called the Albukhary Foundation gallery. I'm surprised that the guide is a young, white woman who looks like she should be working at a cosmetics counter rather than in a museum. She's knowledgeable though, and it gives me hope that maybe if he sees another white person into Islam, he'll realise it's open to everyone.

The gallery is amazing, there are beautiful artefacts from various phases of the golden age of the Islamic Empire, like a calligraphy display, and an intricate vase with beautiful geometric patterns. I had no idea Islam had contributed so much to art and maths and science. I keep looking over at Darren, who seems to be more focused on me than on the exhibition though I can't deny that I love the attention. He comes alive when we get to the astronomy section.

"Wow! What's that?" Darren heads towards this massive brass disc.

The description label says it's called an astrolabe and was used for calculating the position of the stars.

"This thing is really cool," he whispers to me.

He asks the lady how it works and I'm only half listening, but I'm happy to see him so into it. The tour guide also seems to really engage with him; he talks to her for quite a long time. It's kind of annoying how she keeps touching his arm. I feel like someone's poking daggers into my chest. I can't take it, so I go and look at some of the other stuff, like a beautiful spherical incense burner, engraved in Arabic. I can't have been looking at it for more than a few minutes before I feel a tap on my shoulder.

"Hey, what are you looking at?"

I turn to find him smiling brightly at me. "Why don't you tell me what you learned?"

"Oh, just stuff about that astrolabe thing."

"Like what?" I ask.

He shrugs, a playful smile dancing on his lips. "Just that they used it for navigation and stuff. I can't remember now; I was sort of distracted—I didn't know where you'd gone."

Well, this was not the plan at all! He was supposed to pay attention so he could learn about Islam.

"Come on, let's go see the mummies now," he says.

"Sure," I sigh, defeated. I had imagined him coming out of the tour inspired, asking a million questions about Islam, and wanting to convert, not going on about mummies and eye sockets. This hasn't gone the way I wanted it to.

He reaches out, entwines his fingers with mine, and gives me a slow smile that makes me feel breathless.

Oh my god, who am I kidding? This *so* is a date!

CHAPTER SIXTEEN

I look at my Ten Steps and okay, it hasn't gone exactly to plan. It seems like I'll have to think outside the box to get Darren to go for step two—Shafqat Aunty's Eid Mela. It's an annual family fair and it's always ages after Eid for some reason, maybe because everyone's so exhausted from Ramadan. Judging by how things went at the British Museum, I'm not sure how into it he's going to be, but at least at the British Museum we got to spend the day together.

He made me laugh all the way back telling me how much he hates the history teacher because she keeps pronouncing Muslims like muslin. I thought it was just me that noticed. He couldn't stop smiling on the journey back and his laugh, and the smell of him, made me feel so alive, like I was high on something. He even shared his super-fancy chocolate from the museum gift shop with me too. The best bit was, he followed me on Instagram. I'm a bit mortified that he's going to see I only have ninety-eight followers, but at least I'll get to check out all his posts and stories now.

Maybe the trip hasn't been a total disaster, and to be fair he did talk about how cool the astrolabe was, and that he was totally going to incorporate it into his history essay, although he mainly kept going on about how great the mummies were.

How am I going to bring up the Mela on Sunday? It's not exactly glamorous, but it's fun. I should entice him with all the free food, like Mum's samosas. No one can deny that Mum makes the best samosas ever.

When I next see Darren in school, it's in the history lesson. We hand in our essays to Miss Dawson at the end of the class. When Darren hands his in, he says, "You know, miss, Aisha and I worked really hard on this essay. We even went to the British Museum to research it."

"Oooh!" whistles Jason. "Hot date was it, Aisha?"

My cheeks go red.

"Ignore him." Miss Dawson shakes her head. "I'm really glad you're taking this seriously. I'm sure it will reflect in the work; I'm looking forward to reading it."

Darren grins at me while Jason mutters, "Try-hards," under his breath.

I follow Darren out.

"Trying to get brownie points?" I tease.

"You're not annoyed, are you?" he asks.

I'm not annoyed but what if our date gets back to Isabelle?

"Of course not," I say, even though I'm slightly freaking out that she's going to find out.

We go outside to the field and sit on the grass opposite the science department. The scaffolding on the building shields us from curious stares.

"What are you up to this weekend?" I ask. "There's a charity fair that my Aunty is organising, and we're short of volunteers. Would you be interested in helping? You'll get free pizza and samosas."

Please Allah, let him go for it.

"Aisha are you asking me out again?" he teases.

"What! No," I splutter. "I never asked you out before either." I feel my ears burn.

Darren laughs. "Chill, when is it?"

"Sunday lunchtime. It's not hard, all you'll probably have to do is help me sell samosas."

"Alright," he says.

Really? I had a whole speech prepared to try to win him round.

"I need some stuff on my UCAS form. Some charity stuff—it's like a wilderness at the moment."

Oh! So that's why he agreed.

He peers at me. "You know, Aisha, if you want to ask me out, you can just ask me out. You don't have to make up all these elaborate excuses." He nudges my shoulder, a cocky smile on his face.

My face is burning, the nerve of him. "Oh, here we go again, don't flatter yourself. We *are* short of volunteers, it's as simple as that."

"If you say so." He laughs again. "So, your family will be there, right? Have you thought about who you're going to say I am?"

I pause for a moment. "I'm going to say the truth, obviously, that you're my friend."

I haven't thought this through. I haven't considered the impact of him meeting my family—will they be able to tell that we like each other?

"Okay, if you say so." He glances over my shoulder and waves at someone. I turn and see some boys that he plays football with calling him over. Darren stands and brushes the grass off his trousers. "I've got to go but send me the deets for Saturday, babe."

"See you later."

Will my family believe he's just my friend? I know that they're going to be all like, "Why have you got friends who are boys?" or "What are you doing bringing non-Muslims to a Muslim fair?" Maybe this isn't a good idea. I bite my lip and make a mental note to call Shafqat Aunty later. She always has good advice.

Isabelle is walking towards me, munching on a bag of crisps, and I can't quite make out the expression on her face. I hope no one told her about the British Museum.

"Alright, Aisha? Want a crisp?" She offers the packet to me, and I shake my head. "I saw you with Darren. Did he say anything about me? Did he say why he blew me off at the weekend?"

I feel guilty shaking my head. "Why do you care? You said he was creepy."

"He is creepy, I just don't like being blown off like that." Isabelle flicks her hair. "Anyway, when you get a chance, find out what's up with him, yeah?"

"Sure," I mumble, and Isabelle smiles, satisfied.

"Aunty, there's this boy in my class who's interested in helping out with the Mela."

"A boy?" Shafqat Aunty says hesitantly.

"Yes, Aunty, he's not a Muslim, he's a white boy and not very religious, but he seems interested in Islam and all the charity work you do. He really wants to help. I said he can help me sell the samosas."

Shafqat Aunty falls quiet. I bite my lip begging Allah that she won't say no.

"He sounds like a very nice boy," she eventually says. "Yes, bring him. He wants to do good things, that is the main thing. Bring him along, it's fine."

I sigh. I know Shafqat Aunty. The fact that she said it didn't matter that he was white, so meant that it mattered. I really hope they're nice to him. Next step is speaking to Mum and Dad.

They're in the kitchen, Dad is on the sofa fiddling about with his laptop while Mum is making rotis. She's got her checked apron on, there's flour everywhere, and she's sweating from the effort of rolling them flat with her wooden rolling pin. The smell of fresh bread is amazing, though.

"What is it, beta?" Dad asks.

Perfect, he's in a good mood.

"So, you remember they were a bit short of volunteers for the mela on Sunday?" I say.

"No, were they?" Dad barely looks up from his laptop.

"Yes, they were. Well, this white boy from my school is going to help out," I say.

Might as well just spit it out.

Mum turns from the stove, her apron covered in flour, "A white boy! A gora, what gora?"

I roll my eyes. "Chill, Mum, he's from my class. He just

wants to help out so he can put it on his UCAS form, and Shafqat Aunty said it's fine."

"If Shafqat said it's fine, then it is fine. But tell him to make his own way there. There is no space in our car," Dad says.

But Mum is glaring at me. "I don't understand. This is a Muslim function, why this white boy has to come?" She's practically shaking her rolling pin at me.

"Because he wants to help! You should really be more tolerant."

Why does she have to make it such a big deal? How's she going to react when she actually meets him? What would she say if she knew I liked him?!

"Hmph!" She grunts and goes back to making her rotis. She adds some water into the dough and starts kneading so hard I think her knuckles might crack. But I know I've won. Now that Dad has said it's okay, it's definitely okay.

CHAPTER SEVENTEEN

These days all I do is count the days, hours, minutes, and seconds until the next time I'm going to see Darren. The time in between feels like torture. I lay in bed awake thinking about him all the time. I stalk his Instagram, staring at his pictures and posts trying to see if any of them refer to me somehow, but then I'm disappointed that there are no hidden messages, it's pretty much all tennis related.

I post a couple of my best filtered pictures in the hope that he will see them. If he does, he doesn't press like, but it's better than putting it on my story because I know I'll just be obsessing until I see his name appear to show that he's looked at them.

At last, Sunday comes around. I don't know if I'm happy or just nervous—Darren is going to meet my family!

The Mela is being held in a giant field about thirty minutes from our house. I feel bad that Darren has to make his own way there, but he knows it because sometimes the school football team plays there.

We have to be there at midday to set up. At least the weather is decent, the sun's shining and it's warm. Mum and I spent yesterday making a million samosas, and now I'm so tired from stuffing the pastry with meat that I can barely move my wrists. Mum fried them in the morning, and she couldn't understand why I wouldn't help her, but there's no way I'm going to have my hair stinking of grease and fried meat.

Mum and Dad get half a dozen friends to help them lift the giant pots from an Indian general store out of the boot of the car and set up in the stand we've been assigned. I've never seen such large pots and pans anywhere else—they have no handles or a proper lid, just a huge metal plate that sits on the top. Once the pans are in place, all there's left to do is set out paper plates, sauces, and napkins, and the pot to put the cash in.

"You did this last year, didn't you, Aisha?" Dad asks, and I nod. "You can manage with your brothers, can't you? Your mother and I have to help with some other stalls now. Just remember a pound for two samosas, okay? And try to shift all of them."

"No problem."

I'm so glad they're planning to disappear, maybe I can avoid Darren meeting them altogether.

"Where is your gora friend?" Mum says with a sneer on her face. "I thought he was going to help you."

"I'm sure he'll be here soon," I say feeling my cheeks burn.

She's being so rude, but when Darren converts to Islam, she won't be able to complain, because he'll be one of us. No colour or race in Islam—at least that's what Shafqat Aunty always says.

Mum mutters something under her breath and then she and Dad go off to help one of their friends with their clothes stall, quite a way from the food stalls. Good idea, really, I'm sure people don't want to buy clothes smelling of spices.

I'm sandwiched between a doughnut stall and a kebab stall. The air is a strange mix of sweet and savoury smells, and Arabic music is playing in the background. It's such a drag being here early, watching everything being set up before anyone shows up. Burhan and Farhan have a constant eye on the rides.

"As soon as it's ready, let's go," Farhan whispers. "You know it's free for us because we're volunteers."

"You're meant to be helping me!" I remind them. "Why do you want to go on those rides anyway? They look really lame."

There are only four rides. One is a tiny Ferris wheel that only the youngest kids can go on, then there's one with mechanical arms like an octopus, with cars at the end of each arm that go up and down as it spins around, and some really dodgy looking bumper cars. The only half decent ride is the Waltzer, the one that spins until you nearly throw up.

"Who cares?" Farhan says. "They're free. Let's go."

"See ya, sis." Burhan waves at me. "We'll come back when you get some customers."

"Wait—" But they're already running off in their matching T-shirts and shorts.

It's not much fun standing here alone waiting for things to pick up, and where the hell is Darren? I check my phone, but I have no messages from him. I really hope he doesn't bail. I'm faffing around with my phone when Shafqat Aunty walks by.

For some reason, in the open space she looks even smaller and more squished than normal. Sometimes my brothers refer to her as Aunty Squashy-face and today I can see why. She turns to me and beams. All her kindness and serenity seem to flow out through her eyes. She has this vibe where you want to hug her and tell her all your problems.

"Aisha darling, so nice to see you, beta," she says making her way over to my stall. She grasps my hands in hers, and I can't help but think they feel like warm dough. "So lovely of you to help us. All the money will go to those poor children dying in Syria."

I nod. What she says, and the way she says it, puts things into perspective—there are so many things far more important than me and Darren.

As if by magic, as soon as his name pops into my mind, he appears from nowhere. He's striding toward me confidently, wearing a plain black T-shirt and blue jeans. I can see his muscular arms bulging under the material. I feel like running towards him and jumping in his arms but of course I don't. His timing is brilliant though. None of my family are here and I can introduce him to Shafqat Aunty.

"Aisha, mate, I'm so sorry I'm late," he says out of breath. "I had to wait ages for my dad to drop me off." He flashes me a sweet smile and I feel as though something hot and sweet is running through my veins. I see Shafqat Aunty watching me and I drop my gaze—surely Aunty will notice that I totally have the hots for him.

"Don't worry." I release my hands from Shafqat Aunty and motion towards Darren. "Aunty, this is Darren, the boy from my school I told you about."

Darren smiles at her and holds out his hand for her to shake.

She clasps it warmly. "You are the boy who wants to learn more about Islam?" she asks.

OH. MY. GOD!

CHAPTER EIGHTEEN

Can you hear that sound? It's the ground opening up to swallow me whole.

Darren frowns and his gaze flickers from her to me. "I want to know about the charity work that you're doing."

"Yes, that's right," I jump in quickly. "Please tell him all about the charity we're raising money for. All the good work they are doing in Syria."

"Come with me." Shafqat Aunty hasn't released his hands and keeps beaming up at him with that warm smile of hers. "Let us sit and talk for a while."

"Okay," he says, his smile so tight I'm scared his cheeks will crack.

I watch her drag him away to the chai stall and then to a white plastic table set out nearby. Their heads are close together and I wonder what she's saying to him. The expression on his face is strained. I really hope she's not saying I told her that he's thinking of converting to Islam, just the thought makes me feel nauseous. Hopefully, she's just telling him about the charity stuff. I consider joining them to prevent any further damage being done, or at the very least to listen in, but just as I plan to leave the stall, the customers start arriving. Typical!

I smile at the customers and try to ignore the fact that they're staring at me struggling to get my gloves on. I place two samosas in a brown paper bag and am inwardly horrified when I see a huge oil stain appear; I cover it up with some napkins, accept the pound coin, and drop it into the tin we brought with us.

A massive line builds up in no time and there is no trace of Burhan and Farhan anywhere. I faff around with sauces and manage to spill some all over the limited supply of napkins we have. I'm sweating like crazy.

"Alright there, Aisha?" Darren's deep voice comes from behind me. He grabs a pair of gloves and flashes a jaw-dropping smile at the next set of customers. That smile seems to obliterate all my stress and I find myself breaking out into a huge grin.

A bearded man next in line, stares at him suspiciously.

"Assalamualaikum," Darren says politely.

The man's face completely changes, and he beams back at him. "Waalaikumsalam, four samosas, please, brother."

I glance at Darren, and he looks so relaxed as he helps pack up the food. I watch how he delicately puts the samosas into the packet, such a paradox given how muscly his arms are. His hand brushes me lightly as he passes me the pound coin which feels light in my hand. The zing of electricity distracts me from that fact that I really need to quiz him about what Shafqat Aunty said, but there's barely any time as a tsunami of customers keep coming, quashing my hopes for a conversation.

We work hard, squeezing sauces, keeping track of change, dealing with disgruntled people moaning about the amount of oil on the brown paper bags, for what feels like several hours. Although I barely get to talk to Darren, I can't help enjoying being so close to him. We make a good team. It hardly even feels like work. Every so often, our elbows brush, or I see him glancing at me. At one point he leans over me accidentally, but I think it was on purpose, to reach for some napkins. He's so close, I can breathe him in and it makes me feel dizzy. I can't stop watching the way he moves and charms the customers; I fear selling the last of the samosas as I don't want our time together to run out.

Almost an hour later my brothers turn up.

"Decided to show your faces, did you?" I glare at them and whack the top of Burhan's head.

Darren stares at me. "Steady on, Aish, why are you whacking the kids?"

"Don't worry, these are my *useless* brothers, Burhan and Farhan. They were meant to be helping out but disappeared off on the rides."

"Who are you?" Burhan asks, watching Darren suspiciously.

"He's my school friend," I say between gritted teeth.

"Oh, the gora Mum was going on about?" Farhan says and he bursts out laughing.

I glare at him to shut up.

"Gora?" Darren asks me.

"Oh, ignore them. Do you mind showing them what to do?"

My brothers seem a bit off with him at first, but Darren talks to them about football and they soon loosen up and start to banter back and forth. When Burhan makes his first sale, Darren high fives him. It makes me feel warm inside. If we got married, at least he would get on with my brothers.

After a couple of hours, the line settles and we're down to our last few samosas. Finally, a chance to talk! We make Farhan and Burhan do the last of the selling and step back behind the stall.

"Your brothers are cool," Darren says.

"You wouldn't say that if you knew them! They seem to like you, though."

"Can you blame them?" He winks at me.

I pause to clear my throat, but really it's just an excuse to gather up my courage. "What did Shafqat Aunty talk to you about?"

"That lady who took me for chai? She just wanted to tell me how good looking and charming I am, of course."

I laugh. "Cut it out, what did she really say?" I feel sick. Do I even want to know?

"Oh, she was really lovely. She loves *you* by the way—kept going on about what a good girl you are. She was just telling me about all her charity work for those poor Syrian kids. I kept some notes so I can put it on my UCAS form."

Phew, Shafqat Aunty worked her charm on Darren, but then he stares at me, and my heart skips.

"Can I ask you something?"

My throat goes dry. He knows.

"Your Aunty said that you told her I wanted to know all about Islam. Why did she say that?"

I fiddle with my hijab and look away. I can see Burhan and Farhan serving the last of the samosas out of the corner of my eye.

"Oh, didn't you say that?" I feign innocence. "You know, to help with the history module? I thought you wanted to know more about it."

Please let him buy it, please let him buy it.

"Oh, right." He frowns. "But the stuff she was telling me had nothing to do with history. I mean she's a nice lady and everything, but she was kind of preachy, saying that everyone should become a Muslim and believe in God and all that."

I cringe inside.

"But if you do still want to help me with history, do you know what would be really useful?" he continues. I can barely hear him over the sound of the blood rushing to my head. "I really want to see the inside of a mosque. You know, one of those big ones with a dome and that. I swear I saw a question about the history of Islamic architecture, and if I actually saw what one of those fancy mosques looked like, I feel like it would help."

I can't believe it; he's come to point three all by himself! Allah really *is* on my side.

"Yeah, sure! How about we go to Regent's Park Mosque in London? That's got a wicked dome."

"Okay, let's do it." He peers over my shoulder. "Looks like your brothers have sold all the samosas. Does that mean we can go on some of these lame rides now?"

"Yeah, why not. Hey, boys!" I call out to my brothers. "Count up the money and give it to Dad or Shafqat Aunty. We'll be back in a bit."

I ignore the boys' protests. It's my turn to have some fun.

Even though the Waltzer makes me feel sick, I don't think I've ever laughed so much, as I try desperately to stop Darren from spinning the wheel in the middle. I swear he's doing it on purpose so that we can tumble into each other. When we stumble off the Waltzer, barely able to stand, I see Shafqat Aunty smiling warmly at me, but next to her is Mum and she's glaring at me and Darren.

"Hey, Mum," I say, trying to walk in a straight line. "This is my friend Darren, the one I was telling you about."

"Hello, Aunty, nice to meet you." Darren holds out his hand for her to shake.

Mum just about acknowledges him with the curtest of nods. I'm glad he didn't try the Salam thing with her—maybe he sensed it would go down like a lead balloon.

His phone buzzes, and Darren checks the message. He sighs. "Aisha, that was my dad, he's here to pick me up. I've got to go."

The timing's about right, the Mela is winding down, and judging by Mum's face she clearly doesn't want to see him any longer than she needs to.

CHAPTER NINETEEN

The week drags by slowly. The only time I feel alive is when I see Darren at school or at the bus stop. We chat and flirt nearly every day. One morning, I don't see him at the bus stop, so I have to travel alone, and it feels like I've suddenly become invisible the entire journey.

Saturday comes around, and I've told Mum I'm going to Regent's Park Mosque with a friend, which is all the information she needs. I know she won't approve of me seeing Darren again.

The mosque isn't exactly close to the tube, so we have a good ten minutes' walk from Baker Street. I'm wearing my light-coloured blazer again with the list of Ten Steps in the inside pocket.

As we walk along the wide pavements, closely following Darren's navigation on his phone, I start feeling overwhelmed by the amount of people crowding the street. Different languages weave in and out of each other as we bump shoulders with tourists and angry Londoners. To my left are a group of French girls in tiny, denim shorts with huge backpacks on their backs, beside two Arab ladies dressed in Jilbab, who are talking on their expensive mobile phones.

"People seem rich here, don't they?" I say, watching them.

"Don't speak too soon," Darren replies as we approach a pedestrian crossing.

He gestures toward a group of women who are sitting on the floor with their hands out. One lady with coarse brown skin approaches us and starts speaking in a language neither of us understands. She's wearing a black headscarf with silver sequins, and a dirty-coloured floor-length skirt and cardigan.

Darren doesn't even glance in my direction before placing a few pound coins in her hand. The lady bursts into tears as if he is the first person to treat her like a human being—which maybe he is. Before I even have a chance to think about it, the green man flashes, and the crowd carries us forward into the park entrance. I look back at the lady and she's still crying, sharing her bounty with her companions.

When he notices me looking back, he smiles as if it were nothing. Once he's a Muslim, he can join me at the soup kitchens and homeless shelters where Shafqat Aunty and I volunteer.

We enter the park and it's like stepping into a Disney movie. There's a huge lake to the left with white swans swimming in pairs. The flowers are in full bloom, so perfect an artist might have painted them, and giving off an intense sweet smell. Bushes border the paths, peppered in flowers that I've never seen before, and the dappled sunlight is trying to break through the leaves in the trees.

I catch Darren's eye and he's already looking at me. The way he watches me makes me feel like I'm the most beautiful girl in the world. I blush and drop my gaze. As we approach the Mosque, I prepare to be dazzled, but I'm disappointed that the golden dome is faded and not well cared for. A lot of the panels are stained and blackened with dirt. Darren's face falls but he doesn't say anything, and our mood soon lifts once we enter the gates that lead to the Mosque.

"Is it how you remember it?" Darren asks.

"I've never actually been here before," I confess.

"What?"

"I know as much as you do. When you said you wanted to visit a mosque, I suggested this one because I wanted to come too." *With you*, I add in my head.

"Oh my God, Aisha." He laughs. "You should have told me this is your first time here, I thought you were going to be my tour guide."

We climb the steps to the entrance, and in front of us is a large square filled with people. Even at the entrance the men and women are separated, chatting in different groups.

What will they think of me walking in with a white boy? What if someone recognises me and tells my parents? I know I shouldn't care, I'm not doing anything wrong, but still—I can't help gazing around just in case there's someone here I know.

"Did you bring the skull cap I gave you?" I whisper, hoping he'll get the hint and put it on.

"The topi?" He pulls it from his pocket. "I did. See, I'm learning."

He places the cap on his mop of brown hair, and suddenly he looks like a Muslim. It's funny how one simple addition can make someone look completely different, and in fact change their whole identity. I can't stop staring at him. He doesn't seem to notice my reaction as he stares at the huge glass panels which are the windows of the mosque. Through them you can see the amazing chandelier which dominates the interior of the building.

"Wow," he gasps. "That's really beautiful. Let's go inside."

"You know that when we go in, I will have to separate and go to the women's section?"

He nods.

We walk across the square and enter the mosque. There's a huge, tiled lobby, and a shop opposite the entrance with bright lights and books on displays. People are walking purposefully to the various prayer rooms.

"Shall I meet you out the front after the lunchtime prayers? Let's say forty-five minutes?" Darren suggests.

I nod, fascinated by how much he knows. Maybe my plan is working after all. Maybe he is starting to take Islam seriously.

He disappears through the large double doors and I catch sight of the huge, carpeted area that makes up the men's section. The chandelier shimmers and reflects the light in every direction, making it feel like we're inside a treasure chest.

I find the entrance to the women's section and follow directions that lead me up a flight of stairs to the washroom. I take my shoes off and put them in the carrier bag I brought with me. I need to make wudu and enter the huge bathroom fitted with special platforms so I can sit and wash my feet properly.

I smile at whomever I see, and they all say "Assalamualaikum, sister." Everyone is so welcoming. Once I'm done, I walk to the gallery and enter the prayer room. I immediately feel at peace when I go inside. The carpet is designed so that each rectangle is a prayer mat. On either side of the walls are shelves containing books—Qur'an I assume. I can't quite make out the text, but it seems to glimmer in Arabic.

I cross to the gallery overlooking the men's section and lean over trying to spot Darren. I hope he's okay and not feeling too overwhelmed. The men's area is huge, and I can't make him out anywhere.

"Sister, take your place, the Zuhr prayers are about to start," a lady with an Arabic accent says.

I find a space to sit and soon the Imam starts the prayer. It's an amazing experience—the Imam's pronunciation of the Arabic is beautiful, much more poetic than at our local mosque. I feel at peace, transported far from my humdrum life and into a spiritual world that takes me out of myself, almost like a form of meditation. I think of Darren downstairs listening to the prayers, and I pray to Allah, *please make him feel you.*

CHAPTER TWENTY

Once it's over, I find Darren standing in the paved area outside the mosque. He's next to an old man with a beard in a light blue Kurta pyjama and brown waistcoat. They're chatting and laughing as though they've known each other for years. It makes me so happy to see how he fits in so well; everyone gets on with him. Mum and Dad would be sure to accept him if they knew he was serious about Islam. My mind skips forward, and I picture us getting married, me in my red lehenga, and Darren dashing in a white Sherwani. Maybe he could even arrive on a horse.

He turns and spots me. I hear him telling the man that I'm the friend he came with and then he rushes over to me. I see the man glance at me, and I look down, just in case it turns out he knows my dad or something.

"Who was that?" I ask Darren once the man walks away.

"I just got talking to him when I was in there. He showed me what to do and explained a few things."

"What, you mean you prayed?" My eyes light up.

"Well, I went through the motions, and I listened to the Arabic. I've no idea what it meant but yeah, it was pretty cool."

"So, you enjoyed it?"

"Well, I wouldn't go that far, but it was interesting. I'm glad we came," he says with a smile.

God that smile.

After the mosque we go to lunch and stumble upon a posh Indian restaurant called Zainab's, around the corner from the mosque. It stands out from the rest of the buildings with its white archways with golden carvings, and grand wooden doors. It's super-swanky inside—crisp white tablecloths with napkins folded into fan shapes. We're both in jeans and T-shirts so I can't help feeling a little underdressed. Darren doesn't seem to care though.

"I don't think I can afford this," I say.

"It's on me," Darren says. At my surprised face he adds, "I want to treat you."

I'm really starting to feel like a princess. He puts his hand in mine and our fingers intertwine. The Asian waiter, who's dressed in a smart black suit with a white shirt and black bowtie—just like they wear in the movies—leads us to our table right next to the window where we can see all the people walking by. No noise from the outside world can be heard, though. It's perfectly peaceful in here.

The menu has a load of dishes that I recognise as Mum makes stuff that's quite similar, even if the descriptions make everything sound completely different. Bhindi is described as a *delicious Okra marinated in an infusion of spices and then delicately pan-fried until crisp and crunchy. £8.50.*

£8.50! Okra only costs a pound to buy! Talk about commercialisation.

I am careful what I order, I don't want Darren to think that I'm taking advantage of him.

"This looks so good." Darren rubs his hands together.

"It's so expensive, are you sure it's okay?"

"Aisha it's fine. I get to spend time with you, which is all I want."

I feel almost sick with happiness. How lucky am I?

He orders from the better part of the menu for us to share: Bihari kebab, bhindi, and biryani, and enough starters for a party of six. I want to ask him what his dad does to explain all this money he seems to have, but I figure there might not be a way to do this without coming across as rude, so instead I ask what he thought about the mosque.

"It was cool."

"I'm so happy you liked it."

He looks down at the table and fiddles with his cutlery. "Can I ask you something? Why did you want to bring me here?"

My stomach is in knots and the list inside my jacket is burning a hole through my chest. "What do you mean?"

"Aisha, come on, you know that I really like you. I was hoping you came up with this trip to tell me you liked me too." He looks hopefully up at me.

"You really like me?" My skin is on fire and the room suddenly feels too hot. I pull off my jacket hurriedly, but as I do, the piece of paper with the list on it falls onto the table. It's crumpled up but you can see the bright colours through the paper.

"What's this?" he asks, and before I have a chance to stop him, he grabs it.

I reach for it, but he snatches it out of arm's reach.

"Why is this so important?" he asks smiling.

It's like everything is in slow motion as he reads it. At first, he looks confused as if he's trying to decipher the words on the paper, but then his eyes narrow and the smile fades.

"W-what is this?" he stammers. "Ten Steps to converting Darren. . . is this for real?"

"No, wait, please let me explain."

"Take Darren to Regent's Park mosque . . ." he reads the words on the page slowly. "Is this why you brought me here? What were you thinking? Why should I? Why *would* I?" His face is red and glowering, and he's shaking his head at me. "You planned all this, didn't you? I thought you were going to say you liked me, not that you wanted to change me!" He stands, dragging his leather jacket from the back of his seat.

"Darren, please, I'm sorry. Please listen," I plead, and he pauses. "I was trying to—I mean I want—" It's like my words are all jumbled, and I can't form my sentences properly. The more I stumble over my words, the more disgusted Darren looks.

"You've got a screw loose." He twists a finger to his temple before throwing the paper so it lands in front of me.

My whole body is shaking as I watch him walk out. How can things have gone so wrong? My chest hurts when I breathe. I need to talk to him. I have to explain. As I rise to run after him, the waiter drops the bill on the table. I look at the figure, lightheaded. It's over sixty pounds! Dad will go crazy when he checks my emergency account; he gets notifications on this app he has on his phone whenever I use it.

By the time I've paid and am outside, I can't see Darren

anywhere. I take out my phone and call him, praying for him to pick up, but it goes straight to voicemail. My ears burn and despite myself, my eyes fill with hateful tears. I'm so stupid, what was I thinking?

When I get home, Mum is on my case straight away.

"Why you are back so early?"

"I don't feel well," I lie. "I'm going to lay down."

I'm surprised when she doesn't question me further and waves me away. I lay on my bed and my phone buzzes. Please let it be Darren! Please forgive me, please let me explain, but my stomach twists when I see it's a text from Isabelle.

ISABELLE: *You won't believe it—Darren asked out Katy this weekend. Why does he like her but not me?*

He asked out another girl? For the second time that day, my eyes fill with burning, stinging tears, and this time I don't bother fighting them.

CHAPTER TWENTY-ONE

I sit at my desk, and my chest is tight with anxiety. I don't know what to do with myself. I tap my pencil on the desktop, and my eyes wander to my notepad; before I know it, I'm writing at the top of a blank piece of paper: Ten Reasons to get over Darren. What was I thinking?

Ten Reasons to get over Darren
1. He thinks I am mad.
2. He hates me.
3. He is going to tell someone what I did.
4. They are going to tell everyone.
5. Everybody will think that I am mad.
6. He is being a jerk.
7. He knows I like him, but he is taking out Katy.
8. He is trying to make me jealous by taking her out.
9. He might have realised he liked Katy all along.
10. He owes me £60.

The list doesn't help much. I'm still stressed and anxious and don't really know what's going on, so I text Isabelle.

ME: *So, what time is Katy's hot date with Darren?*

ISABELLE: *Tomorrow lunchtime, can you believe that he asked her and not me?*

ME: *I really can't tbh.*

ISABELLE: *Maybe he's just doing it to make me jealous?*

ME: *Maybe you were right originally when you thought he was weird . . .*

ISABELLE:*???*

ME: *Because he gets angry so quickly and storms off.*

I erase it immediately.

ME: *What you said about his Instagram page and all that, maybe you were right?*

ISABELLE: *Yeah, he's weird.*

ME: *Did you tell Katy that?*

ISABELLE: *No of course not. But it's not fair, she gets all the guys. Anyway, she's going to give me all the juicy details after. No doubt I'll have to hear her gushing.*

ME: *Okay keep me posted.*

ISABELLE: *GTG I'll let you know what happens.*

Maybe it's for the best anyway. I've done a great job in scaring him off, that's for sure. He clearly thinks becoming a Muslim is the most frightening thing ever. Or maybe he was just freaked out—he said that I was trying to change him, and I know I was, but it's only so we can be together.

"You know how I feel about you, Aisha."

I keep replaying Darren's words in my head. I look down at my hands and I realise I'm touching the sections of my thumbs where his hands caressed mine. How long does it take to get over a boy? Why can't I stop thinking about him? I've ruined everything. This hurts so bad my chest physically aches every time I think about what happened. My ears burn, and I squeeze my eyes shut, trying to block it out. And now he's taking Katy out. Love is really shit.

I wake early the next day, determined not to feel sorry for myself. Taking my mind off Darren means keeping busy, which is what I tell myself as I enter my brothers' bedroom.

"Come on, wake up! Let's go cycling. All you boys ever do is watch YouTube videos."

The boys actually jump out of bed and hurry to get ready. They love cycling. Mum and Dad are still lazing around in bed, so when I tell them our plans, Dad mumbles something about helmets. The boys and I grab some brioche buns from the bread bin, and then go out the back door to the shed in our back garden which is small and mostly paved over because Mum and Dad don't like gardening. I unlock the shed door and pull the bikes out one by one. The boys stand and watch me and I'm soon out of breath.

"For God's sake, give me a hand, Burhan," I say. "You're eleven not two."

"Sorry," he says, not meaning it for a second.

He drags his bike down to the back door and pulls it open. Farhan does the same and we head off. As soon as I'm on the bike I suddenly remember how much fun cycling is. We pedal down the quiet side roads and into the woods which are so beautiful this time of year. It's a gorgeous, sunny summer day with a light breeze—perfect for cycling. There's so much more to life than boys, and it's time I started remembering that.

Kent may not be that diverse, but it's so pretty. I take in the sounds of the birds in the trees, the smell of flowers, and the beauty of the small ponds as we cycle past. We're out for an hour or so, stopping off for an ice lolly at the log cabin on our way back. My brothers' cheeks are flushed from the exercise, and for the first time in ages, I haven't thought about Darren once.

That afternoon, I try to kill the rest of the day by focusing on my homework. Dad's always saying what a good girl I am going upstairs to study. If only he knew how much time I waste on my phone and laptop and daydreaming about Darren. At this rate, I'll never get into university. Oh my God, how awful would that be? Imagine if I was stuck in this town for the rest of my life. I have to go to London. It's way more diverse and vibrant, and there are so many brown-skinned girls, no one would look twice at me in my hijab.

I keep my phone off to avoid the temptation, and manage to stay strong until four, when Darren and Katy will be well into their date. When I switch it back on, there are dozens of WhatsApp messages—separate ones from Darren and Isabelle.

What on earth?

First, a whole chain of messages from Isabelle.

12:30. *You will not believe it. Darren blew off Katy at the last minute—said he doesn't want to lead her on. . .*

12:35. *He told her like one hour before they were meant to meet, pretty rude, right?*

12:37. *OMG! He told her he likes someone else! Do you think it's me???*

12:50. *Should I call him?*

14:00. *Why don't you ever look at your phone? I need a friend—where are you when I need you?!!*

And a whole chain of messages from Darren too.

12:00. *I'm really sorry about yesterday.* :(

12:01. *I behaved like an idiot.*

12:02. *I guess you heard that I asked Katy out, but I've cancelled. I was just doing it to make you jealous, but I know that's wrong, and not fair to you or her. I think we should talk.*

12:05. *Will you forgive me for walking out of the restaurant like that? Do you think we can talk?*

12:45. *I guess you're still pretty mad because you're not answering.*

13:30. *I overreacted. I am interested in learning more about you and that includes your faith—can we talk?*

He wants to learn more about my faith! What?! I haven't lost him. Oh, my God! I can't believe it. Only thing now is, what am I supposed to reply to both of them?

CHAPTER TWENTY-TWO

I'm about to call Isabelle when Darren's number flashes up. I hesitate for a second before picking up.

"Aisha, finally! Listen, I need to talk to you." He's speaking fast, barely taking a breath between words. "I'm sorry for walking out like that. I was. . . shocked, and I reacted badly."

"I know I freaked you out, but you left me in the middle of that restaurant, and I had to pay the bill! Have you got any idea how humiliating that was? And then I hear you asked Katy out and messed her around too. What are you playing at?"

"I'm sorry, I'm sorry. I'll pay you back, I promise."

His remorse sounds genuine, and the truth is, none of this would have happened if he hadn't seen my plan. Maybe I should never have made the plan in the first place.

"I'm sorry too," I whisper. "I guess I just—I don't know, I thought . . ."

"Look, can we meet up? I really want to talk this through. I want to understand your side of things, and I think it would be better if we spoke in person."

I want to meet him. I hadn't realised until now, how scared I was that he would never talk to me again, but he has some amends to make too. What excuse can I make today when I already went out yesterday? Mum and Dad are bound to get suspicious because I never normally go out this much.

"We can talk after school tomorrow if you want?"

"Okay, that sounds good," he says.

"See you tomorrow."

I hang up and I can't stop the grin from spreading across my face. He wants to give us another chance. I can't believe I freaked him out that much, yet he still wants to see me.

"Aisha, what are you doing in your room all the time alone? Are you still studying?" Mum calls upstairs. "Can you come down and help me?"

"I'm coming," I say.

After making me hang up the clothes, sweep the floor, and put the dishes away, Mum makes me watch a Pakistani drama with her. She says Dad and my brothers are not interested, and what's the point of having a daughter if she spends all her time in her bedroom alone.

I groan and give in, not so much because I don't want a fight, but also because I secretly love Pakistani dramas. Each one is like thirty episodes long and ridiculously slow, but the characters feel genuine, and their struggles are so realistic I feel like I can identify with them. Today's drama has a young couple fighting about some stupid misunderstanding. You can tell they're totally made for each other by the passion in the way they fight. The girl's gone off to her mother's in a huff.

"I loved him a lot," she tells her mother.

"Then why don't you bend?" her mother says. "In love there are no calculations. Remember the branch that bends is the one full of fruit. The branch that is upright is barren and alone."

It makes me think about me and Darren. He's willing to bend and so am I.

I try playing it cool at school and wait for Darren to find me, but Isabelle seeks me out and asks me to go to the tuck shop with her at breaktime.

"I am so over that guy," Isabelle moans as we stand in line. "I called him yesterday and asked him why he cancelled the date with Katy, and if I was the girl that he was interested in."

"No way!" I could never be that ballsy.

"He said he just sees me as a friend. Can you believe it?"

Even though I already know, I still feel relieved. "What did you say?"

"I said that's fine, of course. To be honest I don't think I really liked him anyway. It's only because he was new, it was just the novelty of the whole thing." She scowls and pushes the hair out of her face. She pauses for a moment, her lips quivering. I know how much she liked him.

"How's Katy?"

"Oh, she was so mad. She said he kept going on about some other girl he likes. I don't know who this mystery girl is, but we both reckon he just made her up, cos hello, where is she?"

I wonder what she would do if I said she's right here.

"So, you're cool with it all?" I ask slowly.

"Yes, totally! In fact, I've got my eyes on a new guy."

Already?

"Who?"

"Jason from the rugby team, much more my type."

"Jason from my history class?" I ask, and she nods. "Well, I'm sure he fancies you."

"He better! I don't look this good for nothing." She laughs, but when I don't join in she adds, "I'm kidding, Aisha."

Kidding or not, I wish I had her confidence.

Isabelle and I head to lunch together and I spot Darren. He drops his gaze to the table but a minute later my phone buzzes.

Meet me at the bus stop after school at four-fifteen.

I've already told Mum I'll be home late after school—study group is my excuse—but I've lied to her more times in the past few months than in my entire life. Who am I becoming? Isabelle's going out with her mum after school, so she won't spot us. The bus stop is a good location because no one will question us both being there, we're just trying to get home.

When Darren arrives, he links his arm with mine, and we start walking.

"Where are we going?" I ask.

"There's a café around the corner. It's not very nice so no one really goes there, but we can talk in peace."

The café is run down, with a weathered sign hanging above the door that reads 'Delice'. Brown paint is peeling off the outside walls, and a crack runs along the window which is still covered in fake snow from who knows how many Christmases ago.

As the door swings open a little bell rings, and an old man with a bald head and gold-rimmed glasses comes to the counter. He looks like he could be an extra from a *Harry*

Potter movie, which fits the style of the place as a whole—it's so old-fashioned, with dated dark wooden tables paired with benches and chairs of the same material that have seen better days. The walls are clad with wood panelling and covered in faded signs and newspaper clippings in dusty frames. There's no one else in the place which suits us both fine.

"What do you want to drink?" he asks.

"Hot chocolate and a cheese toastie, please."

When he comes back from ordering, he sits opposite me and takes out his phone. "Let me ping across the money I owe you. Give me your details."

As soon as I text it over, he transfers the money instantly.

"It was supposed to be my treat, I'm so sorry again. I should never have behaved that way with you. That list—it freaked me out. I was confused, but I realise getting Katy involved was wrong." He leans forward in his chair. "My head's been all over the place recently but one thing I'm certain of is, I like you."

I swallow. "I like you too. . . and I'm sorry."

"It's not your fault. I should have let you explain. I know you have no bad intentions, so I should have been more open to hear you out. The truth is part of the reason why I like you is because you're so sincere and brave. So, I've been thinking, and I want to know what that whole step-by-step plan was all about."

"Really?" I ask, surprised.

Darren smiles. "Really."

Without looking directly at him, I say, "I just thought that if I could get you to understand more about Islam, we could . . ."

"We could what?"

"You know. . . date, be together, whatever." My skin is burning hot as I say the words.

He breaks into a huge smile. "Ah, okay, now I see why you were so passionate about it. You could have just told me that from the get-go. So, unless I'm Muslim, you can't date me?"

I shake my head.

"So maybe we shouldn't give up on the steps then."

What?! Not only has he forgiven me, but he's willing to let me keep moving forward with my plan? Allah is *so* on my side. This only confirms that I'm meant to help Darren on his journey to becoming a Muslim and then we can be together.

"I'm not saying I'm going to convert to Islam for definite, but I'm open to learning. I'm doing this for you, Aisha, but this has to be a two-way street."

I frown. "What do you mean?"

"I mean I want to learn all about you and your religion, but you have to learn a little about me too."

"Yes, of course."

Darren reaches across the table and holds my hand, rubbing his thumb across it.

I know I still need to explain that if he became a Muslim, we could be together but we can't be intimate unless we're Islamically married. Sure, he fancies me, but what if he doesn't feel as strongly as I do. Would he be okay with waiting? I don't dare ask. I couldn't take it if he said no and that's the end of us.

Everyone always goes on about how great love is, but what no one ever tells you is how it's hell when you find it what with all the pain and uncertainty, the constant questioning of everything—I only hope Darren and I are worth it.

CHAPTER TWENTY-THREE

Shafqat Aunty turns up for lunch wearing a white salwar kameez that brightens up her soft features even more than her gentle smile naturally does. When I see her, I instantly feel guilty. How can I look her in the eye after all the lies and wrong things I've done?

Thankfully, I don't have to worry too much as Mum and Shafqat Aunty gossip over a huge lunch of biryani and vegetables, dal and roti, without paying much attention to me. We gorge ourselves on Indian sweets and rice pudding and relax in a contented heap over tea in the afternoon.

I'm building up to ask her if she knows any reverts that I can introduce Darren to when she suddenly bursts into tears.

"What's wrong Shafqat?" Mum asks, grabbing her hands to comfort her.

"It's my daughter, Zeba," she says. "She wants to divorce her husband."

"What?" Mum gasps. "Why? She only got married a couple of years ago, didn't she? And the baby Zeeshan, he's only six months old!"

"The man we arranged her marriage to, Sameer, he is not a good man." Shafqat Aunty sobs. "Zeba always told me that she didn't want to marry someone from Pakistan, but we couldn't find anyone from here. But after only one week of marriage, he punched Zeba in the face for not cooking food properly."

Mum and I exchange a look, both too stunned to speak.

"I don't know why he is like this," Shafqat Aunty cries. "He is an educated man, with a good job, and we thought he was from a good family, but he gets so angry."

Shafqat Aunty tells us that she and her daughter Zeba had hoped things would settle down, but they haven't. There are periods of quiet, but after a few months, something makes him lose his temper and nothing can stop him from taking it out on Zeba, not even her pregnancy.

The more details Shafqat Aunty reveals about the living hell her daughter is in, the more sick I feel. I can't imagine how Zeba must be feeling, how desperate she must be.

"Last weekend I had to drive to their house to collect the baby," Shafqat Aunty says. "Zeba was crying so much. Sameer had left the house after hitting her, and she wanted me to take the baby away. I was so worried she was going to do something to herself, but she just didn't want the baby to see her like that."

"Well surely Zeba should get a divorce, shouldn't she, Shafqat Aunty?" I say. There seems no question about it; the husband sounds like a monster, and neither Zeba nor her child should stay where they are in danger.

"You be quiet, Aisha," Mum snaps at me.

"No, it's okay," says Shafqat Aunty. "Aisha, Zeba has a child now, she has a responsibility to him and to his father, however he may be."

"But he beats her!" I say.

"That is her fate," she says, and begins crying again. "It is her bad luck; we are all tested in this life. I never thought my poor girl would have to endure such a harsh test, but if it guarantees her place in heaven, then that is how it must be."

My head is spinning. What the hell? Is this for real? I cannot believe the words that are coming out of this woman's mouth.

"So, you won't support her decision to leave him?"

"She has a child now. I can't support her ruining her life and the child's life."

"Aisha, will you settle down?" Mum glares at me. "These are grownup matters. You go away from here for a bit and play with your brothers. You do not understand these things yet."

Play with your brothers? Did she really just say that? I storm out of the living room. It's all I can do to not scream at them both. I can't believe I looked up to this woman who would let her daughter get beaten and do nothing? Does she really hope that will earn her a place in heaven? It sounds more like she's just letting a tragedy in the making continue its course. I'm glad I haven't asked her about Darren. God knows what kind of rubbish she would have come out with then. Worst of all, Mum seems to agree with her, and that terrifies me. Does that mean Mum would marry me off to anyone, as long as they're Muslim, and I just have to hope for the best? If the guy beats me, well, I have to see it as my ticket to heaven!

There's no way I'm ever going to have some tick-box arranged marriage and take that kind of risk. I'm not going to be the girl who takes a good beating and puts up with any old crap, and I won't have to—I've got Darren.

Later that day, Darren texts me to ask what the next step of the list is. I don't tell him it's to introduce him to reverts, as that will mean having to ask Shafqat Aunty if she knows any, and I've decided I'm not speaking to her ever again. The next best thing is to read the stories of famous reverts, like the ones I found when I was doing my research, so I suggest we do that.

To my surprise, Darren invites me to his house the next day so we can look at the stories together.

And now, here I am in Darren's bedroom. Alone, just me and him.

CHAPTER TWENTY-FOUR

"Don't worry, no one's here," Darren says when he catches me looking uncertainly around the room. "My dad works till really late, and my grandma has gone to stay with my aunty for a few days."

Darren's bedroom is large, and his signature Lynx fragrance lingers in the air. There's a desk with a lamp screwed onto the side against the wall, a shelf above it with a stack of computer games, and a box of wires and plugs and stuff. The walls are empty and painted a shade of off-white that reflects the light, except for one wall which has a single poster of the Wimbledon tennis logo.

"You really are a big fan, aren't you?" I say.

"I love it." He goes to the poster and touches it.

I pretend not to notice how he seems infinitely sad suddenly, and before I get the chance to ask if he's okay, the smile is back on his face.

"So, shall we look at these stories then?"

"Before we do, why don't you tell me some stuff about you? You said this should be a two-way street and I agree."

"Okay." His eyes light up. "Do you want to watch a tennis match then?"

"Huh?"

"Wimbledon is on right now," he says grabbing my hands. "Nadal is playing, he's in the middle of a match literally as we speak. What do you say?"

I have no clue who Nadal is, but I'm sure I'll find out soon enough if this enthusiasm is anything to go by.

"We are going to read about the reverts together though?"

"We will after, come on, let's watch it on my laptop." Darren drags me over to his bed and we sit side-by-side so we can both see the screen. I can barely breathe from how excited I am about being this close to him, but if he feels the same, he certainly doesn't show it. He goes on iPlayer, and we catch the last thirty minutes of the match. I know the basics of tennis, as in, the point is to hit the ball over the net and not let it get past you, but it's never really got me going the way Darren seems to be into it.

He keeps shouting stuff like, "Did you see the spin on that? The guy is a total genius." I nod along, not quite sure what he's so excited about. He watches all the post-match interviews with this huge, animated grin.

"Do you see how much class Nadal has? Look how he never disses his opponents, even if it's a total douchebag like Kyrgios."

I nod along. "Kyrgios is the annoying Australian guy, right?"

"Yeah." His eyes don't leave the screen. "So, what did you think?" he asks, once it's over.

"Yeah, it was great," I say. For a moment, I wonder if this is how he felt when I took him to the British Museum, when I was so clearly into it, and he wasn't. "What's your favourite part about it, though? Tennis, I mean."

His eyes light up. "I love the psychological aspect—it's like a chess game. One on one, a total mental battle. These guys, they know exactly where to place the shots, so the other guy has to run. They work it out, it's all logic, not just brute force. And the thing about Nadal, about all the champions, is that even when they're down, they don't give up, they dig deep, work out a solution to the problem. Do you see what I'm saying?"

He's so into it, it's adorable. I can't help but smile.

"Have you ever been to watch it live?" I ask.

I don't realise what I've triggered until the words leave my lips. He goes silent for a moment. He doesn't look at me and puts his hands in his hair.

"What?" I say, searching his face. "What's wrong?"

He looks up at me with those hazel pools of pent-up feeling. I fear my heart might just break at the sight.

"I used to go with my mum. We used to line up every year, get up at the crack of dawn, camp out. She was the one who got me into it."

I'm such an idiot. No wonder it means so much to him.

"It must have been wonderful to share that with her. I've never been to Wimbledon. You must have the best stories about it."

"I have pictures that I can show you if you want?"

"Yes please." I nod.

"I feel like you're the only person I can share these memories with."

My face flushes. He makes me feel like the most special girl in the world.

He fumbles around under the bed for the albums and

while he's doing that, I stare out of the window at the massive garden—overgrown and uncared for. Between his dad working so much and him taking care of his grandma and doing schoolwork, it's not surprising it's in such a shameful state.

He eventually pulls out the album from under the bed; it's covered with dust which he wipes with his sleeve, and from what I can see, some of the pages are falling out.

"Do you not look at it much?" I ask.

He shakes his head and then starts turning the pages. The first picture is dog-eared and faded but is of a pretty blonde woman in a hospital gown holding a baby. She looks tired but happy.

"Is that you?"

"Yeah, I was pretty cute, wasn't I?"

"Yeah, you were."

"What, am I not cute now?" he teases.

"Not at all," I giggle.

We turn the pages, and there are a series of photos with Darren looking ridiculous in dungarees and woolly hats, growing taller with each page. The pretty blonde woman looks radiant in each of them, especially the ones where they are standing outside Wimbledon Centre court. He must have been five or six in the first one.

Darren keeps flicking through the pages and adding details, sharing anecdotes of the time he let go of his mum's hand and thought he'd be lost forever, only to find her two minutes later, or when he got sunburnt and she bought him ice cream to make up for it.

When we reach the last page of the album, there's a photo of his mum in a hospital bed again, but this time her face is gaunt, the joy completely gone from eyes. I can tell she is trying to smile but her efforts fall short of successful.

Tears well in my eyes. Why the hell am I crying? It was his mum, for God's sake but somehow, I can't stop.

Darren gently wipes the tears from my cheeks "You okay?"

"It should be me consoling you, not the other way around. You must miss her so much."

He nods and a pained look comes back to his face. "She was an amazing person you know—could never bear to see anyone in pain."

"I'm sure she would be very proud of you."

I place my hand on his and squeeze his fingers. He looks at me and before I know it, he moves forwards and his lips are touching mine. Oh my God! This is actually happening. It would be romantic if I wasn't so stressed. Am I even doing it right? His lips are soft, and he is pressing them against mine. Do I shut my eyes? Or keep staring at him? I don't want to freak him out. Where am I supposed to put my arms?

He pulls back and smiles. "Aisha, just relax."

"I'm sorry." I can feel my face heating up. "I've never done this before."

"Yeah, I can tell."

I didn't think it would be possible, but I'm even more mortified now.

"Let me give you a tip," he says, a smile on his lips. "You have to look up and stare into my eyes."

I do and it feels so intense.

"Aisha, do you want to kiss me?"

I nod.

Before I know it, we're kissing again. He pushes his lips

into mine, fiercely. I try shutting my eyes which seems to help; I've waited for this moment for so long. The sweet anticipation of hands I know will touch me soon. How many times have I dreamt about this? About kissing these sugar lips and having his fingers touch me? And now it's actually happening and it's a thousand times better than I could ever have imagined. This moment can't be thought about, it has to be felt. Suddenly, he pulls back.

"What's wrong?" I ask. My eyes snap wide open.

He leans forward and brushes the hair out of his face before covering it with his hands altogether.

"I dunno, I feel odd. I'm just making sure you really want to do this." He glances at my headscarf.

I run my hand over it feeling the familiar soft texture. The headscarf is a part of me; I forget it's even on. I try not to think about how it's meant to be a sign of modesty. To be honest, all I can think about is how great that last kiss felt. I've never known anything like it, and I don't want it to stop.

"I'll take it off," I say, and Darren's eyes widen.

I walk towards the full-length mirror on the side of the cupboard by the door, and look at my reflection, mainly to work out where my pins are so I can take it off easily. My hands tremble as I fiddle with the pins. My hair is tied up in a ponytail underneath and the whole thing is a bit cumbersome. I want the hijab off as quickly as possible, then I can go back to kissing Darren without any restrictions. When the scarf drops to the ground, I stare at it briefly, but I'm so caught up in the moment, I don't allow myself to dwell on the seriousness of what I've just done.

Darren is still staring at me and this time, I take the first step and move forward. But he pulls back again.

"Slow down," he says. "I've never seen you without your scarf before; let me look at you for a moment." We're sitting on the bed together, just the tiniest distance between us. "Wow!"

I want him to want me even more. I reach to the back of my head, pull the hairband from my ponytail, and my hair cascades down my back.

"You're so beautiful." He gently strokes the side of my face before moving slowly towards me and our lips find each other again.

I want to push into him further and harder and feel him envelop me. My body tingles all over and I want him to touch me everywhere. We are breathless when we eventually pull apart. He circles my lips with his fingers and gives me the softest of kisses before resting his forehead against mine.

"You're amazing," he whispers.

The dreamlike daze is interrupted by a text message on his phone.

"Sorry, just a sec."

As he reaches for his phone, I glimpse my reflection in the mirror, and shame washes over me. My hair is a tangled mess, my cheeks are flushed, my eyes are dilated like a drug addict, and my hijab is on the floor. My lips feel swollen from kissing so much. I came here to help him with his journey to Islam, but instead I kissed him.

What am I doing?

CHAPTER TWENTY-FIVE

"Sorry about that, Aisha." Darren puts down his phone and leans towards me. "Where were we?"

I push him away. "I'm sorry, I need to go."

I stand up, pick my hijab up off the floor, and start putting it back on. In the mirror, I can see him walking towards me as I hurriedly tie my hair back.

"I don't understand. What's wrong?"

"I just changed my mind." I pin my hijab back in place and turn away. I can't even look at myself anymore.

"I'm confused, one minute we're kissing and now you're running away. What's going on?" He comes towards me and gently smooths a strand of hair that's escaped from under my hijab. He whispers in my ear, watching me with those huge puppy dog eyes. "I know you're confused, Aisha, but I do really like you. If you need more time, I understand."

Why does he have to be so nice and understanding? It would be easier if he was horrible, then I could just forget about him, and I would feel none of this torment. I grab my stuff and start making my way out. He follows me down the stairs and all the way to the front door.

At the door, I hesitate. "You won't tell anyone what happened, will you?"

His face falls, and he rubs at his forehead. "No, of course not. How can you even think that?" He pauses for a moment. "Do you want me to come with you to the bus stop?"

I shake my head and get out of there as fast as I can.

All the way home I keep thinking, why did I kiss him? What was I becoming? It was all haram, but it felt so good, and I know that if we hadn't been interrupted it would have gone further. I shake my head, disgusted with myself, especially because I know I'm going to do it again.

I'm desperate to tell someone about what happened between me and Darren. I can still taste his kiss on my lips, but who can I turn to? I can't tell Isabelle, she'd be furious with me, and so would Shafqat Aunty. Perhaps she's psychic, because later that evening while I'm on my bed daydreaming about Darren, she sends me a message.

SHAFQAT AUNTY: *Aisha darling how are you? Are you still angry with me? Can't we talk? Let me explain things.*

At first, I want to ignore the message. She betrayed Zeba, so how can I trust her? But then I think maybe she's misguided and I should hear her out. I know she's not a bad person even though I don't agree with her choices. I hold my phone for ages, mulling things over, before I dial her number. She picks up straightaway.

"Aisha darling is that you? Assalamualaikum, beta, it's so nice to hear from you."

"Walaikumsalam, Aunty. You want to speak to me?"

"I am your friend Aisha, and I know you are angry, but maybe we can meet and discuss things? What do you say, beta?" Her soft honey voice draws me in.

I so want to see her, there is so much on my mind, and I could do with a friend. Pausing for a moment I say, "Okay."

We arrange to meet the next day in a coffee shop in the town shopping centre. When I arrive, she's already sitting on a sofa. She waves me over, warm kindness beaming out from her saggy face. I make my way towards her and she stands, reaching for me with her warm dough-like hands.

"Aisha, assalamualaikum, how are you? Tell me what you want to eat. I will go and order."

"Walaikumsalam," I say. "No, Aunty, let me go and line up."

She nods, presses twenty pounds into my hand and tells me she only wants a cup of coffee. The place is noisy with the hum of conversation and the hissing of the various machines. The noise distracts me from my thoughts. For the first time in our relationship, I worry that our conversation will be awkward.

I walk slowly back to the table carrying the tray with a cheese toastie, hot chocolate, and coffee, and do my best not to spill any but it's tough, and some of the hot chocolate spills onto the tray. I sit down and Shafqat Aunty straightaway starts mopping up. I offer her the change, but she shakes her head and refuses to take it.

"So, what did you want to talk to me about, Aunty?"

She leans forward and places her soft hands in mine which are warm from holding the coffee. "Please explain why you're angry with me."

"Why won't you let Zeba get a divorce?" I ask.

She smiles at me and tilts her head to one side. "Aisha, you're so young. I know it must be hard to understand. Have you ever heard this statement 'The most detestable of lawful things before Allah is divorce?' Marriage is a sacred thing and must not be broken lightly. Zeba and Sameer must try to make the marriage work."

I shake my head. "I know that, Aunty, but he's hurting her, and it sounds like she has tried with him. Maybe now it's time to finish it."

"You are so westernised," she says sharply. "That is why you think like this."

I hate this. Just because I object to domestic violence, she's calling me westernised. What's next? Will she accuse of me being a coconut, brown on the outside, white on the inside?

"You're the one making me westernised," I practically spit the words out. "Can't you see this kind of talk is pushing me away from Islam?"

"Aisha, keep your voice down," she says, looking around, but no one is paying attention to us. "What do you mean, you are turning away from Islam?"

Aunty asking me to keep my voice down makes my temperature rise even more. She has asked me why I'm turning away from Islam so I'm going to tell her everything. It's all her fault anyway.

"Yes, that's right, Aunty. Do you know I kissed a white boy yesterday? I couldn't fight the temptation anymore." As soon as the words escape my mouth, I know I've made a mistake.

CHAPTER TWENTY-SIX

"You kissed a white boy?" I can tell by her expression that those are the only words she catches. "Was it that white boy you brought to the mela?"

I nod. Oh, my God, she is so missing the point. "Yes! But, Aunty you are not listening to why I did it."

She doesn't hear me. "Aisha, I will have to tell your parents; what you have done is haram."

"Aunty no! Please, you can't do that. They'll be furious. Plus, Darren wants to become a Muslim so—"

She laughs. "He doesn't want to convert, silly girl! He is just trying to get you to do sinful stuff with him. Of course your parents will be furious! Shaitan the devil is leading you astray. What you have done is wrong."

No, Darren did mean it, didn't he? But he wasn't excited to learn about the reverts like he was about watching Wimbledon and kissing me. Oh God my parents cannot find out. "What do you think they will do?"

She purses her lips. "I don't know, Aisha, they will be very upset. They may even send you to Pakistan." She sips her coffee slowly.

"Pakistan!"

Mum and Dad wouldn't do that to me. They're not like that. She's just trying to scare me—or is she? What if she's right? I can't go to Pakistan and be married off to a stranger. That cannot happen.

"Aunty please, I'm begging you. Please don't say anything. What can I say to make this right? I'll do anything."

She takes her time setting her coffee cup down and wiping her mouth delicately with a napkin. "You must promise never to see that boy again, do you understand? If he is at your school, you avoid him. He is Shaitan, leading you to hell."

I nod. I'll just tell her I won't see him, how will she know anyway?

As if reading my mind, she says, "I want you to message him now and explain, then I want you to block his number. You take him off all the Facebook and other things like that. Do you understand?"

She's so cruel! Why is she doing this to me? I get my phone out and text Darren in front of her.

ME: *Darren, I'm so sorry but I can't see you again. My aunty found out about us and she is threatening to tell my parents. I am scared they will send me off to Pakistan. We must avoid each other from now on. I hope you understand.*

I show Shafqat Aunty the message before I send it, but she's not happy.

"Hand me the phone," she says.

I pass it to her, and she adds at the end of the message:

What we have been doing is haram (wrong). It will lead me

to the hellfire. I am sure you don't want that. Please leave me alone.

She shows it to me, and without asking if it's okay, she presses send. I feel like my whole world is crumbling. She fiddles with the phone a bit more and then says, "I have blocked him and deleted his phone number, and I have deleted your social media." For an old lady, she's pretty tech-savvy from all the charity work she does.

Tears escape the corners of my eyes and drip slowly onto my cheeks. I grab a napkin from the table and scrub the tears away.

"Why did you send that? You didn't even give him a chance to respond."

"Look at you," she says, shaking her head, a small smile on her lips. "Why are you crying over a gora? Forget him, go home, and do namaz. Beta you are looking at me as if I'm the enemy. I'm doing this for your own good." She drains her coffee. "I take no pleasure in this, but I promise you I will tell your parents if you ever see this boy again. Trust me I have eyes everywhere."

I should have realised she was evil—only an evil person would force their own daughter to stay with someone that beat them. Why did I ever agree to meet her? I suppress the urge to tip the contents of my untouched hot chocolate onto her lap. I can't believe it's over between me and Darren—maybe we never stood a chance. The shooting pain in my chest feels like my heart is physically breaking.

When I get home, my hands are shaking so badly I can barely get the key in the front door. What if Shafqat Aunty has already called Mum and Dad and told them about Darren? What will they do? What will they say? Will they disown me and send me away? I can't believe the message Aunty sent to Darren, it was so out of order; but he knows me, maybe he'll realise it wasn't me who sent that message. Please Allah, help me!

What if she tells my parents though? What if they actually do send me to Pakistan and marry me off, and I end up with some old cousin with hair sticking out of his ears and nostrils? I've not been to Pakistan for years; I don't know what it's like anymore. What if I end up in some village in the middle of nowhere, not allowed to go out without a male chaperone and resigned to a life of cooking and cleaning. My life will be over! Should I find my passport and hide it somewhere?

Dad looks up from his laptop when I enter. If he knows anything it doesn't show in his face. He's sitting on the sofa in the kitchen while Mum is rolling rotis and is covered in flour. The boys are in the front room playing football on the PlayStation. Everything seems normal. I breathe a sigh of relief but then the phone rings. No one ever rings the landline. Maybe it's Shafqat Aunty ready to snitch on me.

I freeze while Dad answers and all I can hear is, "No. . . no. . . not interested." He slams the phone down and shakes his head. "Stupid cold callers."

I sigh with relief.

He pats me on the head affectionately. "Are you okay, beta?"

"Yes, all good, Dad." I flash him a warm smile. "I'm going to go upstairs. . . err. . . to do some studying."

Dad peers at me over the top of his glasses. "Such a good girl." If only he knew what I was really like.

Mum looks up from her cooking and says, "Why don't you learn how to make roti? When you get married, you will need to know how to do it."

Why does she say that? Calm down, Aisha, Mum's not that subtle. If she knew, she'd be having a major meltdown right now.

"Leave her, she said she has to study. Let her go upstairs," Dad says.

They don't know, I'm okay for now, subhanallah.

I know that Shafqat Aunty said kissing Darren was haram, but it hadn't felt like that. I know it's wrong and we shouldn't be doing it, not until he's a Muslim and we're at least Islamically married but kissing him was amazing. I keep thinking about it, the taste of his lips. It's stirred up all these feelings in me. I so want to do it again and again. But I can't, I've got to at least try and be a better Muslim. I was trying to lead Darren to Allah, but somewhere along the way we both got led astray. I have to try to get back to Allah and stay away from him. . . but how?

He's in my history and chemistry classes—there's a whole lot of chemistry between us, that's for sure. I can't change my classes or drop out to fit in with Shafqat Aunty's rules. If only I could call him and explain, but I'm too scared to call him in case she somehow finds out. That lady is not to be trusted. She didn't even care that I was crying, all she did was stare at me with her blank eyes and say, "Look at you, crying over a gora. . . you should do namaz." Is this what everyone would think if we were together? Maybe I should pray? I need guidance.

I pray Asr and as I say the words in Arabic, I beg Allah to please not let my parents find out and to help me stay away from Darren, but even as I kneel and bow down, thoughts of Darren keep popping into my mind. His lips, the feel of him, the yearning. Why can't Allah just make it go away?

CHAPTER TWENTY-SEVEN

Monday morning is a nightmare. My heart is in my mouth the entire way to school. I take the earlier bus, so I won't see Darren, but I keep finding myself looking around for him anyway, but he isn't there. When I get to school, I rush to history class avoiding eye contact with everyone and keep my head down. He comes in and sits a few rows back from me, and it feels as though his eyes are boring into the back of my head.

After class, I see him hanging around the doorway, laughing and joking with Jason, acting like everything's normal, like he isn't even bothered.

When he sees me, his normally warm eyes are cold. "Alright, Aisha, can I talk to you for a minute?"

"Just for a minute," I say.

Jason gives us both a look as if to say, what's going on here?

We walk to the trestle tables outside where it's a bit more secluded.

"What the hell was that message?" he hisses when we're finally alone and sitting opposite each other. "I couldn't even reply because you blocked me. Why would you do that?"

"My Aunty made me send that text. She found out about

us and is threatening to tell my parents. She said they might send me to Pakistan if they find out," I say, my voice breaking with every other word.

"Are you serious? You don't really think your parents would do something like that, do you? They seem chill."

"But they're not," I say. I can barely even look at him, I am so scared about what would happen, if anyone found out.

I remember Mum commenting once about a distant cousin of ours who did end up being taken to Pakistan and about how she deserved it, because she was doing haram things like smoking weed and dating boys.

"How did your Aunty find out?" he asks.

I sigh. "I told her. I was angry with her," I add quickly when Darren looks at me, surprised. "Her daughter's getting beaten up by her husband and Aunty believes she should stay with him because good Muslim people don't get divorced."

"What? That's so messed up. But what's that got to do with us?"

"I blurted out that she was turning me away from Islam because she won't help her daughter. . ." As soon as I say the words, Darren's face falls.

"Oh, so is that why you kissed me? You were using me to rebel against your Aunty. And now I'm leading you to, what did you call it—hellfire?"

I shake my head. "No, no, I didn't mean it like that. I kissed you because I wanted to. I want to keep seeing you, but I can't risk being caught and shipped off abroad."

He runs a hand through his hair. "This is so bad, Aisha. I don't get why your Aunty is being like this. I mean, can't we just talk to your parents, explain things? I'm sure I could talk them round."

"No way! They'd be furious. Please, I don't want to be sent away."

He stares across the school field, lost in thought. "Is it really that big a deal, you seeing me?"

I chew my bottom lip. "It really is."

"Look, if you're that worried about being sent away, why don't we speak to one of the teachers, see if they can help? They can't do this to you."

"Please, Darren, just leave it, I think it will make things a hundred times worse."

His suggestions are making my head pound. If he carries on like this, he's one hundred percent going to end up getting me shipped to Pakistan.

"You do realise this is tough for me too, don't you? It's like you're ashamed to be seen with me or something."

"It's not like that, she's threatening me."

"And you can't stand up to her, or to your parents? I would do it for you."

"It's too risky," I say. "I thought you'd understand."

"So, what are we going to do then?"

Tears sting behind my eyes. "We just have to avoid each other," I say.

"But I don't want to do that. I want to keep seeing you." He reaches out to stroke my cheek, but I lean backwards and his face falls.

"Maybe Aunty's right, that what we were doing is wrong. I must try to be a better Muslim. My faith is important to me too."

"Oh, I see, and I suppose I'm leading you astray." He pounds his fist on the table, and I jump. "I said I wanted to learn about your faith. We can't just ignore our attraction to each other, Aisha; we wanted to kiss, and I don't regret it. But you know what, if you want to act like nothing happened and avoid me, that's fine. Let's do that then if it makes you feel better."

"I don't want to! I have no choice."

He shakes his head like he doesn't believe me, like he's disappointed that I won't do anything to put this right. "If you say so. Don't worry, Aisha, I'll leave you alone."

He stands and walks off without a backward glance, and I'm left all alone.

CHAPTER TWENTY-EIGHT

The next two weeks are torture. Every time the landline rings at home, I'm convinced it's Shafqat Aunty calling to tell Mum and Dad everything. One night, the phone rings and it is her. I find myself trembling as I try to eavesdrop on their conversation.

"Shafqat, how nice to hear from you," Mum says. I pretend to read my book although I don't even see the words, but luckily the conversation is only about different ways to make chana.

At school, Darren goes to great lengths to ignore me. He must be taking a different bus because I never see him at the bus stop anymore. When I see him in school, he avoids eye contact. Part of me wishes he had ignored everything I told him and tried to be with me anyway, but instead, he hangs out with his football mates, laughing and joking with them as though he doesn't have a care in the world.

Sometimes I see him hanging around with Jason from the rugby team and Isabelle. When I see them all together, I feel stabs of jealousy in my chest, wishing I could join them. The only silver lining is that Isabelle is dating Jason now.

Isabelle doesn't understand why I won't join them for lunch when Darren is with them, so I lie and say Ella and Susie from chemistry asked me to have lunch with them even though they didn't. Then I have to go and find Ella and Susie and ask if I can sit with them. Luckily, they're really nice and are happy for me to join them. We mainly talk about schoolwork and universities we want to apply for.

I resign my days to focusing on my lessons, avoiding Darren, and studying in the evenings. I must forget him and how his lips felt on mine, the way my body tingled every time he touched me. The physical desire to be with him is the hardest thing to fight.

We must fight the nafs, fight our desires, I keep telling myself again and again.

Why did I have to meet him? I was doing just fine on my own till he turned up. Why did he have to arouse all these physical feelings in me and make me fall in love with him? Everyone goes on about how great love is, but it's awful, painful, like being tortured.

I didn't even think love existed, not for girls like me. I thought I would have an arranged marriage like everyone else from my community, and now that I've been forced to stay away from him, I probably will. I'll just have to pretend that I love whoever I marry because they tick all the boxes, but how will I do that, when I've experienced real actual love? Home alone, that's my life now. Resigned to staring at textbooks for all eternity. I'm so fed up that I pick up my chemistry textbook and throw it at the wall. The only social life I have now is going to Asian functions with my family. The next big social event looming is some wedding for some girl I haven't seen for years who is getting married to some guy I've never even heard of. Great.

It's been years since we've been invited to an Asian wedding, which is why when we got the fabric-covered, glitzy invitation in the post, Mum was quick to say, "Yes thank you, we are definitely coming."

The wedding is in Wembley and the long car journey trapped between my brothers play fighting is every bit as awful as I thought it was going to be. Mum forced me to wear a crazy blue outfit that is way too flashy for the occasion—for some reason she thought it would be fine for me to wear a metal breastplate which makes me look like some kind of warrior princess. I might as well be carrying a sword and shield with me to complete the look.

By the time we reach the venue, we're starving. I'm not only nervous about seeing these people I haven't seen for years, but Shafqat Aunty is probably in here somewhere too. I still haven't spoken to her since the coffee shop incident and I'm not sure what I'll do if I see her. Will she cross-question me about Darren? Will she say anything to Mum and Dad? I'll have to stay glued to them at all times just to make sure.

When we enter the plush hotel, I'm dazzled by the kaleidoscope of colours. The girls wear bright fabrics in pinks, blues, and golds that shimmer in the artificial light of the wedding hall.

"Aisha," Sadiyah, a family friend, cries. She's around the same age as me and someone I always hang out with at these Asian functions, but never see on a day-to-day basis. "Assalamualaikum! I haven't seen you in the longest time. You look so pretty."

"So do you," I say, hugging her back. She has a dimple in her left cheek and has gone for the subtlest makeup to highlight her big brown eyes. Her gold jewellery glistens around her neck and ears.

"You want to go and see Zara?" Mum asks.

I frown. "Who?"

"The girl who is getting married," she snaps.

I've only met her twice, but I allow Mum to drag me to her. Sadiyah follows us.

We find Zara in a small but very luxurious room being fussed over by all her close female friends. There's a golden sofa and ornate paintings on the wall, and lots of giggling. The rustling of silk saris fills the air. The intoxicating smell of everyone's perfume combined makes my head spin. Zara sits on the sofa wearing an elaborate lehenga. It's traditionally red and encrusted with golden embroidery, her dupatta draping over her head and down her back. It looks so heavy I wonder how she's able to keep her head upright, or how she'll stand with the tons of embroidery and gold jewellery she's wearing. Her face is covered in thick layers of makeup. As a final touch, one of her friends is helping her to untangle the nose ring which attaches to her dupatta, and the massive gold earrings that dangle from her ears.

"Doesn't she look beautiful?" Mum asks.

I nod, and I'm sure I would agree if it wasn't for the look of complete fear on her face.

We go over and say 'Salam' but it's clear she has no idea

who we are, so she just nods politely and thanks us for attending.

"He's coming, he's coming," Zara's sister exclaims, rushing to her side.

"Who's here? The groom?" I ask, confused.

Darren pops into my mind and I glance down at my phone wondering if he's texted me, then I remember that I blocked him, and I'm not meant to be talking to him anyway. I sigh, disappointed.

"No, the Imam of course. The groom is waiting on the stage in the hall. You have forgotten everything," Mum whispers, her disappointment sharp like blades.

"Of course I forgot; I was tiny the last time we came to a wedding like this!" I hiss back at her.

Thankfully, the Imam appears, a youngish man with a serious face and the traditional tidy, well-groomed beard but no moustache. If he had taken a second longer, Mum's anger might have reached new levels.

The Imam sits beside Zara while she places her hand on a Qur'an and asks her if she accepts the marriage proposal. At this point, the women momentarily cover their heads with whatever they can find—their dupattas or the edge of their saris. Zara says she accepts and then that's it, the Nikah is over. Everyone pulls off their head coverings as soon as she says yes, not even waiting for the Imam to leave, and for a moment I wonder why they bothered to cover their heads at all.

The Imam leaves as quickly as he came, and Zara and her mother burst into tears.

"Why are they crying?" I whisper to Mum.

"It's the custom—they are sad because they realise she is actually leaving them."

I can't imagine leaving my family no matter how annoying they are at times, but then if I end up with Darren, maybe I'll never see them again. I shiver at the thought.

We drift back into the hall and watch the rest of the wedding. The Imam obtains consent from the groom who sits on the stage with his father in his sherwani and pugri and looks almost as nervous as Zara. Now they're married, they're allowed to sit together. A Bollywood song plays, and Zara arrives with her entourage of sisters and cousins and makes her way to the stage. Once she gets there, she sits and looks down demurely. The bride and groom don't speak to each other.

I hear someone whisper, "What a joke this shy girl act, they've been dating for years."

It's probably true but why are people so gossipy and judgmental? I picture Darren as the groom, arriving on that stage, tall, and dark-haired. Can you imagine all the mean things people would be saying then? I bet even if he *were* Muslim, they'd still judge him because he's white. But they really shouldn't, it's so un-Islamic. I'm filled with overwhelming gloom. A wedding like this would probably be out of the question for us. That's if he ever talks to me again.

I see Shafqat Aunty. There are so many people, I didn't notice when she arrived, but now she's right behind us. She grabs Mum and gives her a huge hug. We hug next and I wonder if she can feel how tense I am. I used to love the soft feel of her, but now I'm repulsed and want to escape her clutches. I pull away and she frowns at me before glancing at Mum. This is it. . . she's going to tell her.

I force a smile to my face and say in my brightest tone, "Assalamualaikum, Aunty, it's so good to see you again."

She smiles, leans close, and whispers in my ear, "Walaikumsalam, darling, I hope you have been being a good girl?"

I nod. We both glance at Mum who is waving at someone across the room. Aunty places her hand on my arm and says quietly, "Don't worry, I haven't said anything. So long as you are being good, Allah will protect you."

Why do I feel like she's blackmailing me? I hang around Mum, worried that if I leave her alone, Shafqat Aunty will change her mind, but luckily Shafqat Aunty sees some other friends and goes to sit with them.

"I'm just going to see Sadiyah," I tell Mum who waves me away.

Sadiyah's with her mum and a group of ladies I don't recognise. They're looking in Shafqat Aunty's direction. One lady whispers, "I hear Shafqat's daughter wants to get divorced."

"What a disgrace for the family." Sadiyah's mum is wearing a bright green silk sari and she narrows her eyes. "What kind of girl is she? How has Shafqat brought her up, I don't know."

These bloody people! I feel like shouting, *do you know that she is getting beaten up?* But I don't dare say anything. I kind of understand now why Shafqat Aunty feels pressured into making Zeba stay with that awful man—to avoid judgement like this. Doesn't mean it's right though.

I sit down in a miserable daze. I just want to go home.

The delicious smells that waft through the hall aren't enough to cheer me up, but I'd be lying if I said it didn't help to see the waiters appear with the food—starters of kebabs, samosas, and grilled chicken are followed by delicious plates of biryani and vegetable curry. I try eating some, but I feel sick. Mum keeps asking me what's wrong, but it's not like I can tell her, so I shrug in response.

When we finally get home, I go straight to my room. I'm so sickened by what I've heard tonight. How can people ignore that Zeba is being abused? I don't want to be part of this culture anymore; if this is the way people think, then I want out. Darren would never treat me like that. What was I thinking, ending things with him? I don't care who Shafqat Aunty tells. No one can stop us from being together.

Tossing and turning in bed, I see one of my hijabs on the floor. I pick it up, open my drawer, and find a pair of scissors. My blood is gushing through my veins so violently I can hear it, and my face and ears burn. If I could scream without waking everyone up, I would. I start cutting up the cloth. The material rips and tears with each stroke of the scissors. When I've made a large enough rip, I throw the scissors away, and tear up the hijab. The first tear is for Zeba.

Free yourself from that awful man.

The second tear is against Shafqat Aunty.

You might emotionally blackmail your daughter, but you won't blackmail me anymore.

The third tear is against Mum.

I won't be in a tick-box arranged marriage just because someone is Muslim. This is my life.

The fourth tear is for Darren.

I love you and no one can keep us apart.

I rip the hijab again and again, the fabric fluttering around the room like a bird released till there are shreds of black material all over the floor. I sweat with the physical effort of tearing it up. I'm finally going to be free.

CHAPTER TWENTY-NINE

I'm not ready to tell Mum and Dad that I've removed my hijab. I made so much fuss about wearing it in the first place that I'm not up for the interrogation, so I wear a different hijab to school and go straight to the girls' bathroom to take it off. I brush my hair so it's dead straight, focusing on the motion and how the bristles slide through the strands—anything to take my mind off what I'm about to do. How will everyone react?

What will Darren say? Will he understand what I'm trying to tell him—that I want to see him again? I know I hurt him; I only hope he's ready to forgive me. God, why does everything have to be so confusing when it comes to him?

I keep brushing until I'm happy with how my hair looks. It has grown so long recently, almost down to my waist. We have double maths first, so I rush to take my seat before anyone else comes in. Isabelle walks in and is about to take her usual place next to me when she does a double-take.

"Aisha, is that you? Where's your scarf?" she asks, still standing.

"I've decided not to wear it anymore."

I brace myself for the barrage of questions that must be

coming my way but all she says is, "Oh, okay. You'll never guess what happened this weekend!"

She might as well have whacked me in the chest. Can't she see what a big deal this is for me?

Isabelle pushes back her hair and shows me what looks like a bruise on her neck.

"What's that?" I ask peering at it.

"Aisha, you're too much! It's a hickey, of course."

"Yes, yes. I know that," I murmur, my cheeks flushing. "Who's it from?"

"Jason, from the rugby team. The one from your history class." She smiles smugly.

"Lucky you." She is lucky. I wish I could kiss Darren again. I've been dreaming of nothing else ever since the day we kissed in his house.

The maths teacher comes in so thankfully, Isabelle takes her seat, and the conversation is left there. Isabelle keeps flicking her hair back throughout the lesson, deliberately exposing her love bite, and smiling to herself. I notice some boys looking at her neck and smirking, which is weird.

At break time, Ella and Susie ask me where my scarf is, but like Isabelle, they don't make a big deal about it although they do compliment my hair.

Isabelle's talking animatedly to a bunch of girls and showing off her love bite. I keep seeing groups of boys staring at her neck and then at their phones sniggering. What's going on? It's not until lunchtime that I hear the whispers

"Isabelle's done stuff with Jason. What a slut, right?" I see a group of girls pointing and giggling.

Has Isabelle heard?

I can't find her around school, so I search for her in the fields, but besides a few groups of kids from other years, there's no trace of her. The search is made more difficult by people stopping me to ask where my scarf is; thankfully no one says anything mean to me.

When I eventually find her, she's with the popular girls, sitting on the grass messing with their phones and chatting.

"Isabelle, can I talk to you for a second?" I ask.

She looks up and her nose is red and there are tears in her eyes. "Jason's such a bastard, Aisha, he's made up a bunch of stuff about me," she says, her voice broken.

"What's happened?" I kneel beside her and take her hand. "How does everyone know?"

"Look!" She holds up her phone and shows me a close-up picture of her face, clearly visible, and turned to the side exposing a shiny red spot on her neck where the bruise is now. The caption underneath says: THAT'S NOT ALL SHE'LL LET YOU DO. "He posted it on Snapchat."

I wish I knew what to say to make her feel better. "What are you going to do?"

But Isabelle is looking over my shoulder at something. I follow her gaze to where Jason is by the benches with his friends.

"How dare he just *stand* there laughing with all his mates? Like he didn't just destroy my life by lying like that."

Before I can stop her, she jumps up and starts running towards Jason, so fast I don't react until she's several yards away. I'm on my feet and chasing after her. I catch up just in time to hear her shout, "How could you do this to me?"

Jason's tall and broad. Being on the rugby team has

turned him into a wall of muscle, and even though I suppose other girls would say he's handsome, the lack of brains and compassion is evident—right now, he's like the ugliest person I've ever seen. He smirks and makes a jerking gesture with his hand.

The fire in Isabelle extinguishes as quickly as it appeared. She bursts into tears and runs through the field back towards the school. I run after her but she's faster than I thought, and I have to stop in the middle of the field and catch my breath. That's when I see a group of Darren's football mates. He's not with them though.

There are at least five of them, standing around one of the old oak trees surrounding the field. I want to go over and ask them where Darren is; I want to ask his advice about Isabelle. I make my way cautiously over to the group to see if I can catch someone's attention, but I feel awkward because they're all boys.

Sam has his back to me, and I can just about hear their conversation as I approach. They're all staring at their phones.

"Wasn't Isabelle chasing after Darren?" Sam asks. "Seems he missed a freebie if this picture is anything to go by. Jason got in there first."

"Eurgh, that girl is for guys who are too lazy to wank!" Luke laughs.

Is this really what boys think—that we're just pieces of meat, sexual objects to be used and thrown away?

Sam turns around and catches my eye. I can see him taking me in and trying to work out what's different about me. "Is that you, Aisha?"

"Ooh, check you out, sexy," Luke says, and the boys laugh

"You guys are nothing but stupid immature idiots!" I shout and shake my head at them. Tears prick at my eyes, and I storm off.

CHAPTER THIRTY

Poor Isabelle, I have to find her. I try calling her phone, but it's switched off. I can't send her messages on social media so I text her. Where is she? I approach the school building feeling tearful; all that stuff the boys said has made me feel sick. I make my way straight to the toilets to avoid anyone seeing me upset.

Luckily, the bathroom's just been cleaned and smells of fresh lemons rather than wee. No one's there. I catch sight of my face in the mirror; if it's possible, I'd say I look like I've aged several years in just a few hours. I look tired, spent. . . sad.

I enter one of the cubicles, lock the door, put the cracked ceramic toilet seat down and sit on it. Hot tears flood down my cheeks. I had taken my scarf off to be free, but am I any freer without it? My face is covered in snot, sweat, and tears, so I grab some toilet paper to dry it, even if the material scratches my skin. When did my hair get covered in the mix too? My hair! My goddamn hair! Is this why I removed my hijab, so I could get it tangled up with snot? What's the point of removing it if it just gives guys an excuse to objectify us?

I hear the door swing open. Footsteps enter followed by

giggling and young voices: must be the year sevens. I stop crying so no one can hear me.

Where is Isabelle? Why hasn't she answered my messages? Her phone must be switched off, I guess. I was supposed to look for my friend, support her when she needed me most, but instead I've come in here to cry my eyes out. I'm such a shit friend. The time on my phone shows that I'm already five minutes late for afternoon lessons. Hopefully, I'll see Isabelle in class.

"Good evening, Aisha," my teacher says sarcastically when I enter the room late.

"Sorry, miss, I lost track of time," I mumble.

She narrows her eyes at me as I shuffle over to my usual seat. Isabelle normally sits next to me but she's not there and she doesn't turn up the whole lesson. Where is she? The lesson drags and I can't seem to focus; I keep getting the algebra all wrong. The teacher keeps tutting at me saying that today's subject is year eleven stuff and what on earth has happened to my memory. I'm wondering the same thing.

There's a weird atmosphere in the room. It's stuffy and hot because it's summer, but there are dark clouds looming. Through the classroom window, I watch them rolling towards us as though they are going to bowl straight into the school. Before long, the heavens open, and rain is splattering and lashing the glass, so loud it drowns out my thoughts.

When the lesson ends, I leave the classroom as quickly as I can. I need to find Isabelle. I keep checking my phone in case she has replied to my messages—she hasn't.

I need to put my hijab back on before I go home. Why did I take it off in the first place? If anything, the day's events are

God's way of telling me how much protection it gives me. I go into the bathroom, unfold the black material taking my time placing it back on my head, and as the folds of fabric wrap around me, I sigh with relief. Feeling myself again, I take some tissue and wipe off the final traces of eye makeup—the stuff that hasn't been washed off by my lunchtime tears. Sensible Aisha is back.

When I leave the bathroom, the corridors are empty. I make my way slowly to the bus stop. The rain is finally easing off, but it hasn't stopped fully. There are huge puddles everywhere, the passing cars splashing the pavements; I have to keep moving to avoid the splashes, but when a massive truck zooms past there's not much I can do, and my shoes and tights end up drenched with muddy water. As I get closer to the bus stop, I make out a tall, familiar figure sitting on the wall, dripping.

Darren?

I freeze, my stomach all tied up in knots. Hair dripping, and clothes soaked, his navy blue trousers look almost black with the rain.

"What are you doing here?" I ask.

He stands and runs his fingers through his hair, cascading water everywhere. "I've been waiting for you. Look, I know we're not supposed to see each other, but I heard what happened to Isabelle. Can we go somewhere and talk?"

He stares at me like the rest of the world has disappeared. I've missed that feeling so much; I've missed him so much. I can't stop myself from smiling.

"Yes," I say.

I recognise the route to Delice even before the rundown

café appears sandwiched between the other buildings. If the old man behind the counter recognises us, he certainly doesn't show it.

While Darren goes to the bathroom to dry off, I ask the old man to bring us two hot chocolates. I get cream and sprinkles for Darren's one, I know he likes that stuff. I text Mum to tell her I'll be late because I'm studying.

I sit at the dark wooden table with the horrible chairs that wobble. Within minutes the two hot chocolates appear. When Darren emerges from the bathroom, he's changed his shirt and blazer and is wearing his hoodie from his games kit.

He smiles when he sees the hot chocolates.

"Cheers, you shouldn't have."

"We need something to warm you up," I say.

"God, I've missed you, Aisha," he says. He takes my fingers in his. The warmth of his hands sends waves of electricity through me. "Will you get into big trouble for meeting me like this?"

I shrug. "Right now, I don't care." I pause. "I've missed you too, so much."

His face lights up. "I got you this." He releases my hands, reaches into his pocket, and hands me a burner phone. "This way, we can text each other safely."

I laugh. "Are we selling drugs or something?"

"I know, right, it's mad but how else can we communicate with each other?"

"I thought today was just a one-time thing?" I say, batting my eyelashes at him. "We're here to talk about Isabelle."

His face falls. "Sorry, how is she?"

"I don't know. She won't answer my messages. Let me check again." I reach into my bag and grab my smartphone. "Oh, she's answered."

ISABELLE: *I'm doing better. Thanks for asking, babes. I just had to get out of school. I've deleted my Snapchat and Insta for now, was getting so much trolling it was untrue, that's probz why you couldn't contact me. I know you tried to call but I really don't feel like talking to anyone right now. If you want, we can meet on Sunday, wanna come over?*

ME: *I'm glad you're ok. I was so worried. I'll def come over Sunday afternoon x*

She replies straightaway with a smiley face.

"Thank God she's okay," he says.

"You know your mates were saying really awful things about her. Come to think of it, so were a lot of the girls."

Darren sighs and stares at his drink. "I don't know, there's a lot of pressure to be a certain way, especially if you're a guy. Every weekend, people go to parties and get drunk and it's almost like you're compelled to get with girls and boast about it. I'm not saying it's cool, like I know it's really messed up, but I guess they're just idiots. I don't think they get how it affects someone. Plus, she was a bit stupid for boasting about it like that."

"Hey, don't bash my friend!"

He goes red. "You're the one asking why they were reacting like that; I'm just trying to explain."

"But you're not like that, are you?" I say and find myself

reaching for his hands again. In a world that has been so full of tears lately, he's the one consolation.

"No, but there's a lot of pressure to be a certain way, especially from the guys in the football team."

I pause for a moment. I've never thought about it that way, the pressure boys are under. I always assumed that life was so much easier for boys because that's what Mum always told me.

"Anyway, I heard you took your hijab off," he says looking at it. "But it's back on again. What's happening? FYI you look beautiful with or without a hijab."

I blush. I want to kiss him so bad but how can we in the middle of this café. What if someone walks past?

"I don't know, I feel so messed up these days. Shafqat Aunty's attitude towards her daughter getting beaten up just makes me sick. In fact, all the aunties seem to think she should just accept it. It's really made me question my religion. I guess I just thought if I took the hijab off it would make life less complicated."

"So why did you put it back on then?"

"I dunno, I missed it, I guess. I didn't like the way some people were staring at me."

"It's horrible what's happening to your Aunty's daughter. Don't tell anyone this, but I know for a fact that before my mum got sick, my dad slapped her a couple of times."

I gasp. "What? Are you serious?"

"Yeah, it sucks. I think it was only twice, but still it happened." His jaw is clenched, tense. "I don't want to talk about it too much, but I guess what I'm trying to say is, it can happen to anyone. I know I'm no expert, but I don't think all Muslims think like your Aunty and your Mum. I'm fairly sure my mates from Bow don't think like that. You know the guys at this school, they're not my real friends. They're just people I've latched on to because I didn't know anyone. Maybe I can introduce you to my real friends from East London?"

The pictures from his Instagram flash before my eyes—his Muslim friends.

"I wish I could meet them too," I say, and I really mean it. It would be amazing to meet people like me.

"What are you doing on Saturday?" he asks suddenly. "I'm getting together with them and I'm sure they would love you. What do you think?"

Oh God, I really want to go, but I'm seeing Isabelle on Sunday, and my parents will want to know why I'm so busy this weekend. And then there's Shafqat Aunty. Who knows who she's got spying on me?

"I just need to figure things out with my parents and make sure Aunty doesn't find out somehow. How would you introduce me to them?"

He smiles. "Well, I would love to say you're my girlfriend, but I'm not sure how you would feel about that." He leans in, and there's tense electricity between us.

Girlfriend! I would love to claim that title.

"I want to be but . . ."

"I know," he nods. "Friends okay?"

I smile. "Friends would be great."

CHAPTER THIRTY-ONE

Mum is standing at the kitchen sink washing and draining the raw rice repeatedly before she puts it on to boil like it's a sacred ritual. She doesn't need to look up to start having a go at me for being so late. I protest about helping to prepare dinner because I have so much work to do, and she stops suddenly, her beady eyes on me.

"I thought you were late because of studying, so why you still have homework?"

She has a point. Is it just me or is she looking at me suspiciously? Has Shafqat Aunty said something? Her eyes seem narrower than normal, and her mouth has transformed into a tight button. What would she think if she knew I had in fact been spending time with a boy instead of studying? Well, according to Shafqat Aunty she would probably ship me off to Pakistan to marry one of my cousins. I don't know if they would actually do that but it makes me sick just thinking about it. She pulls the edge of her dupatta tightly over her shoulder.

"Hurry up, lots to do."

I go upstairs to dump my stuff in my room but end up faffing around for ages. I come down and ask Mum if she still needs help, but she shakes her head and says, "Too late now, just eat. Your dad and brothers have already had their food."

I sit at the kitchen table and wait. She puts a plate of roti, aloo ki sabzi, and chicken curry in front of me. I break the pieces of roti and form morsels around the rest of the food. I cram it into my mouth and feel instantly better.

When we're done eating I help Mum take the dishes to the sink, I turn to go upstairs. I need a shower and to check my phone, but Mum is blocking the staircase.

"You never talk to us anymore, Aisha. You seem different," Mum says. She's standing in front of me, hands on her hips.

My knees shake and I lean against the wall. What does she know? Why is she saying this? Has Shafqat Aunty betrayed me after all? I take a deep breath.

"What do you mean? I'm just tired, I guess."

Dad must have been hanging around the doorway because he appears as if from nowhere. "Your mother is only worried about you."

He sits back down at his place at the kitchen table and gestures for me to do the same. I know better than to go against him. Mum takes the seat in front of me, and they both exchange a serious glance.

Well, I guess I should dig out my passport from the back of my drawer. Pakistan, here I come.

"You're so quiet these days, always in your room, always late from school," he continues. "Your Shafqat Aunty also says she is worried about you, you never call her anymore."

"Did she say anything else about me?"

"No, just that you're distant with her, like you are with us," Dad says, and I breathe a sigh of relief. But now that I realise they don't know anything, I feel bold enough to say what I really feel.

"Why are you all gossiping behind my back?" I whine. I'm so fed up with everyone breathing down my neck all the time, words tumble from my mouth in a garbled mess. "Have you got any idea how much pressure I'm under? I am doing my A-levels and it's difficult. You say you want me to be a doctor, but how can I do that if I don't study?"

"But you said you don't want to be a doctor," Dad replies.

"Well, I haven't decided yet, have I? But with all this pressure all the time, what else am I supposed to do?" I'm practically spitting the words out.

"No one is pressuring you," he replies calmly, and it's true. I knew even when I said it that it was unfair. "We're all just worried about you."

"Why? What is there to be worried about?"

"I am worried you are becoming a... a..."

"A what?" I say. A slut, a whore, what?

"A fanatic!"

"A fanatic?" What is he talking about? I laugh, a short snappy sound. "Dad, are you for real?"

But he's so deadly serious, my smile wavers.

"I read about these young girls all the time on the internet, looking at these crazy videos and becoming radicalised. And all the time you are on the computer and on the phone, and now you are ignoring Shafqat. She is worried you are under somebody's influence." When he says that I freeze. But then Dad says, "Some brainwashing idiot."

Dad thinks I'm some kind of nut-job terrorist! I can't believe it—he's so far off the track it's impossible not to laugh.

At least it means Shafqat Aunty hasn't said anything more. If he knew that I was ripping up my scarf and kissing white boys, what on earth would he think? Maybe he would sigh with relief—anything was surely better than having an extremist for a daughter. Should I tell him the truth? No, it's not worth the risk.

"Dad, that's crazy. Do you not know me at all? Go and look at my computer if you want, look at the search history if you're so worried."

But then I think about all the conversion stuff I've looked at; he'd probably misinterpret all of it. Dad pauses for a moment and Mum is quiet too. What are they thinking?

"Ok then, beti," he eventually says. "I believe you. I just wanted to check you were okay."

"I've just been working too hard." I'm tired, it's true, but it's so not from studying all the time; it's the emotional drama that's exhausting.

He studies my face for several moments and then he rises and stands closer to me. "I'm sorry, beti," Dad whispers and pats the top of my head.

I smile weakly at him. He smiles back, and I think he's convinced. Ruthlessly, I seize the opportunity to talk about the weekend.

"Could I go to London with some friends this Saturday? I really could use a break from all this studying."

He breathes out slowly and crosses his arms over his chest. "What friends are these and where exactly are you going?"

"I'm going to East London to meet some Muslim girls—my friend from school is going to introduce me to them." I'm not lying, I'm just keeping it vague.

His face breaks into a smile, "Muslim girls, that is very good, very good. Just make sure you are back by eleven pm, beti."

I nod and make a mental note to tell Darren we'll need to meet early enough so I can get home in time. What's happening to me? Dad suspects me of being a terrorist and the first thing I do is manipulate the situation so I can see Darren at the weekend. If I spent half the time I spend lying about studying actually doing some schoolwork, I'd probably be top of the year!

I wish I could be honest with my parents, but after this conversation, I feel like they don't even know me. How could they think I'm a terrorist? What kind of person do they think they've raised—the same tired cliché everyone seems to think all Muslims are? They're almost as bad as the boys at the bus stop.

In my room, I check the burner phone Darren gave me. There are messages from him! I'm so excited I drop the phone twice before I open them.

DARREN: *I'm so glad we managed to sort stuff out. Did you ask your mum about Saturday?*

ME: *They said I could go as long as I'm back by eleven so it would have to be lunchtime or early dinner.*

DARREN: *That's great! We're meeting at two thirty, so that's fine. Can't wait for them all to meet you X*

I send a smiley face, but when I catch sight of my reflection in the mirror, I realise that I'm not actually smiling. The muscles in my face are tense and my eyes are wide. What if they don't like me? What if they think I'm weird? What if Shafqat Aunty finds out and it gets back to my parents, and they really do ship me off to Pakistan?

But I want to spend time with Darren. I'm going to meet his friends and be part of his world. All this time I've spent wondering about the friends in his Instagram pictures, thinking I would never get to meet them, and now it's finally happening! There's no way I'm passing up the opportunity to learn all about the boy of my dreams from the people who know him best.

CHAPTER THIRTY-TWO

I arrive at the station early as Dad insists on giving me a lift. This morning, I swear the whole universe is conspiring against me. I woke up with a massive spot on the side of my cheek which I tried to cover with makeup and only ended up making it worse, and then had to keep applying layer upon layer of Mum's concealer until the red finally faded enough to stop drawing attention to itself.

Then, when I was getting dressed, the seams of my sleeve popped because a thread got tangled on something, so I had to change, but then I realised I forgot to put my dirty laundry in the basket in the bathroom so all I was left with that wasn't school clothes, was an unremarkable black shirt and an old pair of jeans. At least I get to wear my favourite hijab—a beautiful shade that reminds me of strawberries, a rich red that makes my skin pop. I always feel a little more confident when I wear it, and God knows I'll need all the confidence I can get today.

Dad is long gone by the time Darren arrives his usual five minutes late. When he gets closer, I see he's carrying a large brown paper bag. I wonder what's inside. He's wearing his black leather jacket with a white T-shirt, blue jeans, and black boots—he looks like he's the hot lead in a fifties film.

"What's in the bag?"

"Sandwiches for lunch," he replies, waving it.

"Oh," I say, a sinking feeling in my chest. "I thought we were meeting for lunch?"

"No, we're going to Blitz with them for milkshakes and waffles. We can eat lunch on the train."

We have a Blitz in our local shopping centre, and I can go there anytime, but halal restaurants like the ones in East London I've never seen around here. I did some research while I was waiting to leave, and there were so many amazing options, it's a real bummer we won't be going to any of them. I take a deep breath. It doesn't matter. I'm with Darren and that's what counts.

When the train arrives, it's rammed, but Darren manages to find us two seats together. He lets me take the window seat; being so close to him makes the familiar butterflies start up in my stomach again.

"So, who exactly is going to be there today?" I ask.

"Well, let me think." His leg brushes mine sending a zing up my spine. "There's quite a crowd coming, Shazya and Halima and Rowshonara for starters."

"All girls?" I ask and rub my nose to try to hide my surprise.

"No, no, Riz and Dave are coming too."

"Who's Dave?" I ask.

Darren grins. "He was the other white kid in my year—there were only two of us so we kind of bonded over it."

"And the rest are Muslim?" I ask.

"Yeah, I think they're all Bangladeshi though, except

perhaps Shazya, so the girls may tease you a bit. They all think they're better looking than Pakistanis."

That makes me smile because Mum is always saying how Pakistanis are so much better looking than Bangladeshis.

"So, who are your best friends?" I ask, desperately hoping he won't say any of the girls.

"Well, Riz is a really cool guy, good fun, and he helped me a lot when I first started. You know, because of my dad's job, we've always moved around a lot. Dave and I had the white thing which we always laugh about. He's alright, you'll like him, and you know, Shazya and I used to be close at one time."

"But you're not close anymore?" What does he mean *close?*

"Well, I moved here, didn't I?" he says. He stares out of the window as if he wants to change the subject.

"What do you think they'll think of me?" I ask, hoping he won't see how nervous I am.

"Relax, Aisha, they're all chill. I mean, some of the girls wear the scarf, and some don't. Most of the time we just chat about what shows we're watching on Netflix."

We spend the rest of the journey discussing films and music, and Darren goes on and on about Drill and how great OFB are while we eat the sandwiches he brought. I don't dare tell him I spent the morning listening to 'Adore You' by Harry Styles the whole time I was faffing around with my clothes.

We're running a bit late as the train gets held up right outside the station, but I appreciate having a couple of extra minutes just the two of us. What if I have nothing to say, and they all think I'm really weird? Why can't I just relax?

As soon as we exit Whitechapel station, I'm hit by the smell of curry and sweat and oil. It's a sweltering day. We walk along a busy road with cars and trucks zooming past, and a row of market stalls. I can't make out what anyone is saying but it's very loud.

We don't say much as we rush through the crowd. I keep my eyes down, wondering what people will think of me being with a white boy. I'm glad we're walking fast, as the faces and voices all seem to blur around me. This is a first though, being amongst a sea of brown faces instead of white ones, and yet I'm still wondering how they will judge me.

Within five minutes we arrive at the familiar Blitz logo. I peer through the window and catch the eye of a beautiful girl with mocha skin, eyes like a Siamese cat, and glossy red lips, all framed by an elegant pale blue hijab gathered up on one side. Darren locks eyes with her and I pray this isn't the girl he told me he used to be close to.

"Let's go in and meet everyone."

I nod and gulp and hope he doesn't notice that I'm trembling.

CHAPTER THIRTY-THREE

Besides its size, this Blitz isn't too different from the one back home. It has the signature lurid pink sofas and shiny black floors, the aroma of caramel, sugar, and warm chocolate, filling the air and making my stomach rumble.

We make our way up the spiral staircase to the second storey, where there's a huge black rectangular table surrounded by sofas. A glittering disco ball hangs from the ceiling, reflecting sparkly lights back at the group of brown faces and one white, all smiling at us from their seats. A tall Asian boy with black-rimmed glasses, a beard, and moustache, stands. It's more of a hipster than a traditional Muslim look, I'd say. He comes towards us and grasps Darren's hands in one of those 'yo, fam' type embraces.

"Hey, bruv, how are you? It's been ages." He's all smiles and so is Darren.

I stand there feeling quietly tiny between them; the boy towers over me. He says to Darren, "Is this your friend?"

"Yeah." Darren glances at me. "This is Aisha, she's a mate from school."

Is it just me, or has his accent taken on an East London twang?

"Hi," I say and hold out my hand. He stares for a minute, then I immediately lower my hand and blush. I forgot that some Muslims won't—or don't—shake hands with people from the opposite sex. Great! They're all going to think I'm a fake Muslim now.

And then he throws his arms around me and says, "Hi, Aisha, I'm Riz, why don't you come and sit here?"

And just like that the hurricane of thoughts calms down long enough for me to follow him to the table. He guides me to an empty space opposite a pretty Asian girl wearing a pale blue hijab. She's the girl! The one I saw downstairs through the window.

"Shazya!" Darren's face illuminates, his smile stretching from ear-to-ear, and he holds out his arms.

She jumps up and cuddles him. Pangs of jealousy stab me in the chest. This is the girl Darren said he was close to. I feel like my blood's frozen in my veins. I sit at the table while they chat, and I can't quite catch what they're saying to each other, but every so often they glance at me. Eventually she sits back down, and I can look at her properly. She's managed to tie her hijab up the way I've always wanted to where it's all layered on one side and pinned up high on the other. I've tried so many times to do it that way, watched countless YouTube tutorials, and never managed to achieve it. She looks so elegant and poised—pretty much the exact opposite of how I feel.

"Hey," she says. "I'm Shazya." Her eyelids are covered with shimmering bronze eyeshadow, and she's done it perfectly, not a stroke out of place. Liquid eyeliner is on the edge of her lids with an alluring wing at the end, and either she has the thickest eyelashes I've ever seen or she's wearing the most expertly positioned fakes. Her lips are bright red, and her cheeks are bronzed and contoured to perfection. How do I compete with this?

"I'm Aisha," I reply. She sees me staring at her, so I quickly add, "I really like your eye makeup."

"Thanks." She smiles. "That's really sweet."

There's a pause and I get the impression that she's trying to think of something complimentary to say back to me, but she clearly can't think of anything. I tug at the edges of my hijab on one side wishing I'd worn something more interesting or taken Mum up on the offer to borrow her lipstick. I tap my fingers on the table with my other hand.

Darren is now chatting to Riz and I'm waiting for him to come over and sit next to me, but they're talking for ages.

Maybe Shazya sees how uncomfortable I am because she says, "Let me introduce you to everyone." To her right there is a thin dark-skinned girl. She doesn't wear hijab and has long straight black hair. "This is Rowshonara. Rowsh, this is Aisha."

Rowshonara smiles at me briefly and I nod and say hello. The girl on my right also says hi and tells me her name is Halima.

"It's so nice to meet you," she says.

I stare at the empty chair next to me. Darren must read my mind because he comes and finally sits down beside me. Riz and Dave sit to the left of him. I notice Shazya staring at us, her beautiful eyes narrowing a little.

"So, you and Darren go to the same school then?"

Darren nods and I say, "Yeah, we became friends when he moved down to Kent."

"Friends?" she says and arches her perfectly shaped eyebrows.

Why is she looking at us like that? Does she know something?

"Yeah," Darren says.

She smirks before she says, "We've all missed you so much, Darren, haven't we girls?"

The girls all nod.

"It so isn't the same without you," Halima says. I notice how Darren blushes.

An Eastern European waitress arrives with a bunch of menus, and we grab them so fast a couple end up on the floor.

"You know I've been starving myself since last week so that I can have this," Halima says looking proud.

"You look like you've lost weight," Shazya says.

Halima smiles gratefully, "I've lost two pounds this week."

"Oh, you can totally tell," Shazya replies, the sarcastic edge in her voice completely missed—or ignored—by Halima who is still grinning. "Does anyone want to share a waffle?" Shazya looks up and down the table. "There's no way I can eat a whole one."

Halima's lips quiver. "I haven't eaten much all day cos I wanted to have this."

"It's fine, no one said *you* had to share with me," Shazya snaps.

She reminds me of Isabelle, one of those seemingly ultra-confident girls who either don't realise or don't care how much harm their words can cause.

"I'll share with you," I say, trying to diffuse the tension, and Shazya smiles at me.

"Oh, I thought you would share with me," Darren says.

"Dieting are you, Darren?" Shazya teases before I can respond. "Can't handle a waffle now that you're all posh living in Kent."

"Hey, watch it." He laughs. "Okay you two share and I'll prove to you that I can still eat."

"Having the Chocolate Bubblepop Waffle again?"

"What else?" he replies

"Darren never changes," she says to me.

Why do I feel like she's not just talking about the food?

"Well, I have changed a little." He smiles at me. "Aisha, if you want to try it, you can have some. Now tell me, Shazya, would I ever have offered to share my waffle in the past? *Joey doesn't share food!*" He laughs, mimicking the scene from *Friends*.

Shazya leans closer to him. "Can I have some too then?" she asks, giving him a dazzling well-practiced smile.

He shakes his head still grinning. "Nope, only Aisha."

My heart flutters. *Only Aisha, only Aisha,* the words echo around my head. Shazya's eyes slant, and she's not smiling anymore. She obviously still likes Darren.

The waitress arrives with our orders, two of everything on the menu for the boys, it looks like.

"You guys are disgusting," Shazya shouts down the table. "Feeding those spots are you, Riz?"

"Ha-ha very funny! Why don't you tell us what you're hiding under all that makeup, huh?"

The table takes a collective deep breath.

"What a bitch you are!" Shazya says, but she's laughing.

I suddenly remember *my* spot, the one that was stressing me out so much this morning. What if Mum's concealer has rubbed off? I bring my hand to my right cheek and I can still feel it; I'll have to check it in the bathroom later though.

My stomach is tied up in knots again. What if Darren notices my spot? But he's too busy catching up with the boys. The sugary smell of the waffles is making me feel nauseous and I pick at the edges. For all Shazya's moaning, she finishes most of it.

The conversation revolves around their school and teachers, and I feel left out. Darren doesn't even seem to notice as he joins in.

"Is that Mr Tahir still there?" Darren asks. "Is he still going on about the merits of learning for its own sake?"

"Oh God yeah," Shazya says. "He so doesn't get that what motivates us is passing our bloody exams."

"Why don't you beat him up?" Darren laughs. "Are you still doing kick-boxing?"

"She sure is," Halima says. "No one dares mess with her. She's even more fierce than before."

"How do you do kick-boxing with your hijab on?" I find myself blurting out.

"It's not a big deal." Shazya shrugs. "It's a women-only Muslim thing. Loads of girls with hijab go."

"That's the thing," I say. "I'm like the only girl in my school who wears a hijab—in fact I'm the only Muslim."

"Oh, sounds like a real Hicksville where you live. You should move to East London."

I should, I want to, so badly. So much for the submissive Muslim women the media are always forcing down our throats.

CHAPTER THIRTY-FOUR

I excuse myself to go to the bathroom and look in the mirror which is smeared with fingerprints. I'm horrified to see that most of the concealer has worn off, and I'm left with a crusted scab like a lesion in its place. That must have been what Shazya was staring at this whole time. How embarrassing! I unzip my little blue handbag and pull out the small pot of concealer that I nicked from Mum's bedroom. My fingers work rapidly to fix the cracks and within no time I've managed to smooth it all over with a fine dusting of Mum's compact too. I'm putting my makeup away when the door swings open and Shazya comes in.

"Hey," I say, and smile weakly at her.

She nods back. "I see you've got the same idea as me." She pulls out an eyeliner from her handbag. I watch her expertly apply black liquid to the already thickly coated lids.

I go to leave but she steps to one side and blocks my path.

"You're going out with Darren, aren't you?" she says it more like a statement than a question.

I shake my head.

"Oh, come on, Aisha." She rolls her eyes. "I wasn't born yesterday. You know he used to go out with me, but we had to end it when he moved away." Her face has that hard expression again. "You must know he's just using you, right? That he's trying to find a substitute for me."

She eyes me up and down. I know what she's thinking—I'm a poor understudy. I think if she punched me in the guts, it probably would hurt less. Right now, I feel as if I'm being ripped to pieces from the inside out.

"Me and Darren, we're just mates, that's all," I say.

"If you say so but watch him though. One minute he'll make you feel like you're the centre of the universe, the next you'll never hear from him again."

I don't want to hear any more, so I push past her and leave the bathroom. I want to go home. This whole afternoon has been a disaster. All I wanted to do was make some nice new Muslim friends and hang out with Darren, not deal with his weirdo ex.

When I come out of the bathroom, he's standing outside waiting for me.

"I hope you don't mind, but I told Riz about what's happening with your friend Zeba, and how bad your aunties are being. He's quite a religious dude and he told me that what they're saying is totally un-Islamic."

I'm taken aback that he cared enough to ask on my behalf.

Riz is sitting at a side table. I follow Darren and we slide in opposite him. I want so badly to hold Darren's hand under the table, but I have to be content with being squashed up close to him.

"So, Darren has kind of filled me in about what's been happening. He says your Aunty has been saying that domestic violence has to be tolerated because your friend is married, is that right?" I nod and he shakes his head. "She's not right, you know. That generation, they confuse religion and culture. Look, it's a bit difficult to talk here but I've printed out some notes and this leaflet for you. It's all based on Islamic texts. Have a read later, and if you ever need to talk, Darren can give you my number, okay?"

He passes me the leaflet.

"Thank you." I want to read it right this minute, but I see the others watching us from the main table.

"What's going on back there?" Shazya shouts.

We stand to join them.

"Oh, I was just telling Aisha how these guys are my Gs," Darren explains.

"Don't believe a word this guy says," Dave tells me. "He's so full of BS, we couldn't wait to see the back of him."

They pretend to beat each other up and remind me of my brothers—are all boys frozen at nine years old? The pissed-off looking Eastern European waitress arrives with the bill.

"We didn't even ask for the bill!" Riz says looking at it.

"I need to go anyway," I whisper to Darren. "Dad will get annoyed if I don't get home in time."

"Okay let's speed things up then," Darren says.

They divide up the bill and Darren insists on paying for me. I cast a self-satisfied look in Shazya's direction only to find her already glaring at me.

We hang around outside for a bit, it's a large group and everyone is saying their goodbyes in that peculiar way that could continue for hours if someone doesn't break away from the group soon. Shazya comes over to me and even has the nerve to put a hand on my shoulder.

"It was really nice to meet you, babe—we should totally swap numbers."

I can't think of anything I would like to do less, but Darren is standing right there so I agree. I don't want to seem rude. She types the number into my phone and I know that I'm never going to contact her ever again.

"Keep in touch," she says, looking like a predator pretending to be harmless right before pouncing. "And you," she continues, hugging Darren. "You're very naughty, you never text me anymore."

"I'll make sure I do," he says.

I don't know if it's wishful thinking, but I'm pretty sure he pushes her away as fast as he can when she doesn't end the hug. I'm starting to think I might be right—he's probably blown her off and she can't bear to see him with someone else, and that's why she is trying to intimidate me.

We finally leave and head to the tube. I'm so relieved to be out of there, I suddenly realise how hungry I am. My stomach had been in knots the whole time and I barely ate anything. I can't tell Darren, though, he just paid for me, and I don't want him to think I'm taking advantage.

"You're quiet," Darren says, glancing at me. "Are you okay?" He holds out his hand and I grab it, glad to feel its warmth again.

"I think I am now." I smile.

The train is practically empty, which is a relief. Still, it doesn't seem like talking is included in Darren's plans. The minute we're settled, and the train is moving, he leans over and asks, "Can I kiss you now? I've been dying to all day."

His warm breath washes over me and there's nothing I'd

rather do than let him kiss me, but I have to ask him about Shazya. I pull back and he frowns.

"What's wrong? What did I do?"

"Why did you sit me opposite your ex-girlfriend?"

"What? Which one was my ex-girlfriend?"

"Shazya. She told me you guys used to go out but broke up when you left London."

"Shazya said what? Oh, my days! In her dreams. Seriously, she thinks all the boys are in love with her."

"So, you never went out with her?"

He squirms in his seat for a bit and kicks an empty rolling coffee cup with his foot.

"We had one kiss, that's all."

I nod calmly even though right now I feel like needles are stabbing me in my chest. "That's all we've had though, Darren, isn't it?" I shake my head at him.

He puts his hand on my arm. "The way I feel about you is nothing like what I felt for her. The truth is I didn't want to hurt her feelings, so I used the whole moving to Kent thing as an excuse to get away from her. She was a bit obsessed with me and wanted a relationship, but I wasn't really looking for that with her. Once I got over the initial attraction, I found her a bit shallow."

I want so much to believe him and try to fight my jealousy when he says that he finds her attractive. I guess he's just being honest, and at least he saw through her in the end—not easy when someone's that beautiful.

"So why did you say she was okay then?" I ask.

"I dunno, I thought she'd grown up." He shakes his head. "But clearly not if she's lying to you like that."

"I'm just glad you don't want a relationship with her, but you do want one with me." I nudge him playfully, but Darren isn't smiling, instead he's looking at me intensely and I freeze.

"Aisha, I want you to be my girlfriend—what do you say?"

"Yes," I say before I can stop myself. "But we can't tell anyone. Aunty and my parents cannot find out."

He nods in agreement. "So, can I actually kiss you now?"

My smile is so wide that my face hurts. "Yes," I repeat, and he leans into me and this time I don't pull away.

CHAPTER THIRTY-FIVE

I have a boyfriend. Boring old Aisha has a boyfriend!

When I get home, I just want to lay on my bed and think about what happened on the train. I'm tingling all over just remembering it—the buzz of what we did. His soft, warm kisses, the way he touched the base of my back and cupped my face. Thankfully, I was squashed up against the window, so hopefully no one saw me. I'm not used to all that PDA, but I grow hot when I think about the kisses. I can't get those feelings out of my mind but then I remember the leaflet Riz gave me and curiosity wins.

There's a load of statistics about how domestic violence affects women from all cultures and backgrounds, not just Muslim women. Quotes about Allah being against oppression and Allah offering divorce as an option to escape injustice. So Shafqat Aunty and Mum were just talking a load of old crap then, twisting things to suit their own cultural values. It makes me think how I'm twisting things too, to go out with Darren. I can't use religion as an excuse anymore to do what I want to do with Darren, and there is so much more that I want to do with him . . .

The physical yearning for him is growing stronger and

stronger each time we kiss. It's all I think about, his lips on mine, the way it feels, the way I want things to go further. How much longer can I really fight the nafs?

The leaflet disturbs me because it's not allowing me to do what I want to do. The only way I can get round it in my mind is to keep telling myself the issue isn't just my faith, it's also my culture, well at least the culture that I'm surrounded by, and that's what I have to escape. This leaflet is all theory and doesn't reflect what I'm actually experiencing right now. I don't want to read it anymore, so I tear it into lots of pieces and throw it into my wastepaper basket. I'm not going to think about it anymore. I'm going to think about something else like seeing Isabelle tomorrow and helping her through all the drama she's just been through.

"You spent all day yesterday with your friends, now you want to see friends again today?" Mum shakes her head when I ask if I can go see Isabelle.

"She wasn't there yesterday, Mum, she's not been well, so I'm going to see if she's okay," I whine.

"Day by day, you are getting out of control, Aisha." She glares at me.

"Let her go," Dad says. "Her friend is not well, and she should go and check she is alright. It is the correct thing to do."

"You are spoiling this girl."

She seems to spend a lot of time shaking her head at me these days, but at least Aunty hasn't snaked on me.

I used to love going to Isabelle's house when I was younger. It was the only place I could go without Mum and Dad asking me a billion questions. Isabelle's mum was the only other parent who somewhat acknowledged Mum's existence. I noticed she never invited her over for coffee like she did with the other mums, and it was only ever to arrange stuff with me, but she still made an effort, however small it was.

The walk takes me down several quiet roads. The house is only ten minutes away but it's like walking from one world to another. Our street is full of terraced houses with poky bedrooms, but here the houses are massive. They have huge drives with expensive cars parked on them. One house has a massive treehouse in the garden, and I can see the glint of a swimming pool over the fence.

Isabelle lives in an equally impressive, detached house with an electric gate which you have to buzz through on a little number pad to be allowed in. Growing up, the wait between pressing the buzzer and the doors opening, always felt like a test to see if I was good enough to be allowed into their world. It still takes ages but now I'm not nervous. I'm the confident one with the gorgeous boyfriend, and Isabelle is the one in need of comfort.

I slip through the gap the minute the gates part and make my way across the smooth paved floor. The front garden has a pretty semi-circular area with grass and ceramic sculptures in it. On the other side I see their shiny Mercedes and Jaguar parked side by side in front of their garage.

Isabelle's mum stands at the doorway and welcomes me in. She's slim and blonde and makeup-free in her yoga pants. She's never worked, she's never needed to. Her husband is a super-rich banker. She beams at me.

"It's so good to see you, Aisha, it's been ages—how are you?"

"Oh, I'm good, nice to see you too."

I enter the massive hallway and Isabelle's mum shouts up the stairs, "Isabelle, come down, Aisha is here now."

While I wait for her, I take in the gorgeous Persian carpet that I'm standing on, and all the expensive artwork on the walls. There are lush houseplants everywhere. They've always had a cleaner to keep this place looking so immaculate.

Isabelle comes down the stairs, still in her pyjamas—a rundown set she would have never allowed anyone to see her in if the circumstances were different. Her hair is tangled, and she doesn't have a drop of makeup on which is how I know things are much worse than I thought.

"Hey," she says solemnly.

"Hey."

Her mum offers us tea and snacks, but we say no, and I follow Isabelle up to her bedroom.

Isabelle's house is split into three floors and her room occupies the whole third level, in the loft conversion. She has a really cool king-sized bed in the middle of her room, a gorgeous white dressing table and dresser to one side, *and* a huge desk for her to study on. I glance at the expensive Mac laptop.

I think about my poky bedroom and try to ignore the feelings of resentment that rise in my chest. It's only stuff, what difference does it make? It clearly hasn't made Isabelle happy if her face is anything to go by. She's sitting on her bed with her left knee up near her chin. I sit on the swivel-chair near her desk, facing her but keeping my distance.

I want to hug her, but there's more than just a physical barrier that keeps us from being close to each other—my secret about Darren.

"So how are things?" I ask. "I haven't seen you since . . ."

"Thursday," she completes.

Was it really only three days ago? It seems like forever. So much has happened since then—going for coffee in the rain, Dad accusing me of being a terrorist, going to Blitz and meeting Shazya, and the kiss on the train. Life used to be so boring, and now it feels like a whirlwind.

"It's been pretty hellish to be honest. Jason won't return my messages. I keep asking why he posted that stuff, and he won't answer. It's not like I can tell my mum what I did so I just have to keep pretending I'm sick. It's been a nightmare." Her face is drawn and there are lines around her eyes. I've never seen Isabelle like this before.

"I saw that you're off Insta and Snapchat and everything—have people been messaging you?"

"Well yeah, but it's mainly Jason's friends asking me if I can do the same stuff to them and gross things like that. There's a lot of anonymous stuff too telling me I'm a slut-- did you see that?"

I shake my head, but she keeps staring at me like she's accusing me of being a liar.

"You can report it, you know? Tell the school and they can investigate." Even as the words leave my mouth, I know I don't mean it. It's like when Darren suggested I report Shafqat Aunty, it's never going to happen.

"Yeah right," she scoffs. "Then my mum and all the teachers will find out, and anyone else who somehow missed it will know that Jason's saying I did all this stuff to him, even though I didn't. They might believe him. It will make things a million times worse. No, I'm just going to lay low and stay off socials till it's all settled down. People will forget soon, right?"

I nod.

"I'm not going to be intimidated, Aisha," she says, and her determination takes me by surprise. Looking as frail as she does, I wasn't expecting her to have this in her. "Why is it if a boy sleeps with a hundred girls, he's such a hero, but I get a love bite and everyone's making up all this other stuff about me."

I nod in agreement. The double standards are ridiculous. I don't want to tell her what everyone has been saying about her, that she only got the love bite to get attention and that it was her fault for going around boasting to everyone. If it was what she wanted to do, then why not? What's insane is that no one is saying anything about what an arsehole Jason is.

"Don't worry," I say, "I'm sure it will all blow over soon and I've got your back. Hey, shall we do a makeover?" Isabelle shrugs in response. "Come on, you love them, and it will cheer you up."

I can't bear seeing her like this, so vulnerable and unlike the normal feisty Isabelle. She half-heartedly agrees and goes to her bathroom to wash her face. When she comes back, she sits at her dressing table, and I pull over the chair. Her makeup kit would be the envy of any beauty lover—she has the fanciest palettes, brushes, and products, and drawers full of loose powders, lip glosses and lipsticks, contour sticks, bronzers, highlighters, and so many things I can't even find a name for.

We have a laugh watching me make a mess of putting the stuff on. The makeup remover is out so many times I'm convinced more makeup ended up being wiped off than staying on her face.

"I'm glad you came over, Aisha," she says when we're done. "You're a really good friend."

I smile at her, and I'm surprised to find that I too am glad that I got to spend some time with her. It's been ages since we hung out one on one.

"Anyway, it seems like all we've talked about is my stuff. What's happening with you? What's the latest?"

I don't know why I say it, but it's like the words leave my mouth of their own accord. "I have a boyfriend. But you can't tell anyone."

"What?" Her eyes widen. "Who is it?"

"You have to promise not to tell anyone—my parents would kill me if they found out."

"I promise," she says, placing a hand on her chest. "Now tell me, who is it?"

If I had known a bit of gossip was all it took to get the natural colour back in her cheeks, I would have led by telling her my secret earlier. She looks like she's come back from the dead, a bright smile on her lips, and she's perched on the edge of her bed like she just can't take the anticipation.

"It's Darren."

CHAPTER THIRTY-SIX

She stares at me open-mouthed. "Darren? You and Darren are *together* together?" Her gaze drops to the floor and just like that, the excitement that energised her a second ago seems to fade. "But. . . you're Muslim! You're not supposed to go out with boys, are you?"

"That's why I want you to keep it quiet. No one must know."

"So, wait a minute—the whole time I liked him, you liked him too?"

"No," I lie. "Of course not."

I can see where this is going, and I don't like it one bit. She's going to yell at me and fall out with me, and I can't let her do that or she'll tell everyone about Darren. God I was such a fool for telling her.

"We only started talking properly after you moved on from him." She doesn't say anything and I'm not sure I've convinced her. "You won't say anything to anybody will you? My parents would kill me."

"Of course not." She smiles. "Your secret is safe with me."

I'm surprised to see Isabelle at school the next day, as she said she was going to lay low. Not only that, but she's acting like her old self as if she didn't run out of school in tears. She even leaves me to go sit with her other friends at lunchtime.

I can't see Darren anywhere. I'm about to embrace another lunch hour alone when I spot Ella and Susie from chemistry waving at me to come sit with them.

"How's it going?" Susie pushes her wire-rimmed glasses up her nose. "You're wearing your headscarf again?"

"Yeah," I say and touch the edge self-consciously. "I was experimenting the other day, seeing what I felt like without it. I sort of like it better this way for now."

"You should do what works for you," Ella says.

"I swear chemistry is just getting harder, isn't it?" Susie says and I'm grateful that they're not making a big deal about my hijab.

"I really regret taking it but it's my dad breathing down my neck wanting me to go into chemical engineering."

"Really?" I ask. I'm surprised that Susie has demanding parents like mine. "I always thought it was just Asian parents trying to tell their kids what to do. My parents haven't stopped going on about me practicing medicine since the day I was born."

"Oh, same," she says. "They seem to have my whole future mapped out for me. They want me to go to Cambridge and then, I don't know, probably create a new type of environmentally friendly plastic and win the Nobel Prize for science or something. I'm not even any good at chemistry."

"Are you going to do medicine?" Ella asks me. "You don't seem like you want to."

"Probably not. I'm scared of blood and needles; I'd

probably shake every time I gave someone an injection." I laugh. "To be honest, I would love to be a historian or a financial analyst, maybe even go on *The Apprentice* selling my mum's samosas! Who knows?"

"That show is so cheesy, what even are those lines?" Ella says.

"You're fired," laughs Susie, with her best Lord Sugar impression. "Why doesn't he just say, 'Oi, you, piss off!'?"

Once we finish our lunch, the girls are suggesting we go out to the field when I see Darren enter the hall. I want to run up to him and wrap myself around him, but he's with a couple of his mates, and we are at school, so I stay where I am, waiting for him to make the first move. Will he just walk past me? Part of me thinks he should. We did talk about it on the train, how we must keep it quiet.

His walk through the lunch hall seems to take forever, it's like in the movies where everything goes slow-mo and music blares in the background as the coolest, most handsome guy in school walks past and the girls all swoon. Except none of the girls apart from me seem to be affected—can they not see how gorgeous he is? If I'm acting weird, my friends don't seem to notice, and we stand, collecting out stuff ready to leave.

As we're walking out of the lunch hall, he deliberately brushes past me. No one notices, but he stares at me and his hand touches mine for the briefest moment. The waves of electricity pulse through me and I get that familiar pulling feeling in my stomach again. I flash him the quickest smile and scuttle out of the hall, but as I do, I see Isabelle watching me, with an expression I can't read.

When we get to the field, my phone buzzes in my trouser pocket with a message from him.

DARREN: *This secret thing is kind of sexy. Can't wait till this weekend—get you all to myself. I can't wait to touch you and hold you close to me.*

I hope my new friends don't notice my cheeks burning.

The week goes by with loads of flirty texts between me and Darren in the evening and furtive glances during the day. Thank God Darren's been topping up my phone for me, so I don't have to spend hours away from him. If our paths cross it's for mere instants and we pretend not to know each other. It's as if Isabelle is playing the same game. She's been so distant; I would even go as far as to say she's avoiding me. Maybe she's still processing the whole thing with Jason? We haven't had lunch once this week, and we've barely spoken. She never mentions Darren even though I've caught her staring at us in chemistry.

On the plus side, things are going well with Ella and Susie. I regret not hanging out with them more before. We have lunch together practically every day, and they've really welcomed me into their little bubble. Susie's even invited me to study at her house next week, and let's face it—I need it. The end of year exams are coming soon and I've hardly done any revision.

As far as my parents are concerned, though, I've done nothing *but* study, so I need to make sure the results actually match the amount of time I've spent sneaking around.

I should be catching up on homework, but Darren is all I can think about. I spend every evening thinking about his fingers touching me, caressing my face. We have to be close, so close. I want to make him all mine. It's like a poisoned paradise. We shouldn't be dating, it's haram and I should walk away but it's like I can't move my feet. Something inside me has changed and even though I'm scared, I feel like I must do this. He's opened my eyes to this whole physical world that I didn't even know existed, almost like I was in a coma before. I feel like I'm on a rollercoaster ride and I have to admit I love the danger. I haven't prayed once, and I haven't read the Qur'an in what feels like a lifetime. In fact, I've moved my prayer mat and Qur'an into the spare room. If my parents have noticed they haven't said anything. I can't even look at them because every time I do I feel guilty.

On Friday night I get a text from Shafqat Aunty asking if I've been okay and behaving.

Why has she sent me this? It's like she's read my mind and knows what I'm planning to do with Darren this weekend. I want to throw the phone away, like it's been infected with something. I toy with just ignoring the message but I better not, she might ring Mum. So, with trembling hands, I hit the button to call her.

She picks up straightaway, "Assalamualaikum, Aisha. How are you, darling?"

Her sickly-sweet voice makes me shiver; I used to love her soft tones but now I feel nauseous.

"Walaikumsalam, Aunty. I'm good, how are you?"

"Have you been a good girl? You are staying away from that white boy?"

"Of course, Aunty." I force a laugh. "I would never disobey you."

"Well, it wouldn't be me you are disobeying, it would be Allah," she drawls.

I don't want to hear this, so I counter with, "How's Zeba?" I know from Mum that things have not been good.

"Alhamdulillah, things are improving, Aisha. Zeba is still in the hospital, but she will be okay once she is home."

I know that Zeba's husband put her in the hospital; he broke her leg. "Is she still not going to divorce that horrible man?"

"Divorce is not the answer to everything, Aisha. Allah sends us challenges and we must work out how to deal with these challenges—running away is not the solution."

And there it is: her blindness to how serious the situation actually is. If someone is beating you up, I would say running away is a pretty good option! When I hang up the phone, I'm almost glad she rang. I'm pretty sure she hasn't said anything to Mum and Dad, and her stupid way of thinking has given me all the proof I need—it's time to break free.

It's funny because I wrote my Ten Steps wanting to convert Darren, but now I don't even know if it's what I want myself. I would be with Darren regardless of his beliefs. Filled with a renewed energy I decide to draw up another list.

Ten Steps to Aisha's Happiness
1. Kiss Darren loads.
2. Get rid of the hijab for good.
3. Become the hottest couple in school.
4. Hang out with Ella and Susie instead of Isabelle.

5. Finish my A-levels.
6. Apply for a history degree, **not** Medicine.
7. Go to university in London with Darren.
8. Shake off Shafqat Aunty for good.
9. Ditch Mum and Dad if they don't approve of us.
10. Free myself from the chains of rules and religion.

CHAPTER THIRTY-SEVEN

I plan my journey to Darren's house carefully to avoid bumping into anyone I know. My thoughts whirl as I walk to his house, and my footsteps quicken to keep pace with them. He opens the door and he's showered, the smell of coconut from his shampoo making me wish we were on a desert island together.

It seems like ages since I've been in his room. He's cleaned up—all the computer games and tangles of wire have been arranged neatly, and there are hoover lines in the cream-coloured carpet.

"Where's your dad and Grandma today?" I ask.

At the mention of his dad, his face tenses up. "Oh, he's taking my nan to see my uncle today—my dad's brother. They kept trying to make me go, but there was no way I was missing the opportunity to be with you."

We're standing close to his desk, and he stares at me in that intense way of his, as if he's trying to memorise every inch of my face. My cheeks flush and I desperately want to grab him and kiss him, but I don't want to make the first move and seem too keen. I caress the little scar by his left eye.

"You never told me how you got this," I say softly, feeling the little ridged area under my fingertips.

He grabs my hand sending shivers up my spine. "I think I told you that I fell when I was little," he says but he won't look me in the eye.

"I don't believe you."

"Don't you?" He leads me by the hand to his bed.

We sit down, right in the patch of languid summer sunlight streaming through the window. Even the grey walls seem to glow.

"My mum did it," he says so softly that I think I misheard him.

"Your mum?" I frown. "Why?"

"Towards the end, the cancer had travelled to her brain, and she was drugged up to the eyeballs. She wasn't herself anymore—the morphine, it made her loopy. She'd have all these weird hallucinations and was really paranoid like she thought I was dead and would look at me like I was some undead creature, an evil spirit or something."

I gasp. "Oh my God, how did you deal with that?"

"It was a total nightmare. Dad kept telling me not to take it personally, but it was so hard. She would say such mean things to me one moment, and then be nice the next once the drugs had kicked in. Then one day . . ." he pauses.

"Look, you don't have to talk about this if you don't want to," I say.

"No, I want to. I want to get it off my chest." He takes a deep breath. "She was shouting at me saying I was an undead spirit or something like that, and she just lost it big time. I mean I found out later she had some kind of infection and the cancer had spread into her brain, so she was probably delirious, but at the time I hated her. I thought she meant everything she said. Anyway, she picked up her box of medicines and threw them at me, and that's how I got this scar."

"I'm so sorry that happened to you."

"I hate it. I don't want to remember her like that. I want to remember my actual mum who was kind and caring."

"I don't know what to say. I feel so bad."

"I don't need your pity," he snaps.

"It's not pity!" I shake my head. "I just feel terrible that's what you've been through. I'm here because I want to be. . . because I like you." I blush. "I like you a lot."

The annoyed look disappears and his face breaks into a huge smile that make those gorgeous eyes light up. I melt.

"You have no idea how many lies I've had to tell my family to be here. Why would I do that unless I really liked you?"

I lean into him, and we kiss. It feels like all that pent-up frustration is released once our lips touch. This time my hands are not hanging limply by my side, instead they are wrapped around him, exploring the hair at the nape of his neck, and I'm pushed hard against him. I remember how much the hijab bothered me last time, so I pull away and start taking it off. It's one of those ready-to-wear ones and it comes straight off—I've come prepared this time.

He smooths my hair away from my face and kisses me deeply again. His tongue is caressing mine stirring up feelings down below, and I'm getting hotter and sweatier by the second.

"Maybe we should close the curtains?" I suggest.

"Sure," he breathes, and he roughly drags them across, cutting off the light and the warmth from the sun.

Before he can sit back down, my hands reach to grab the base of his T-shirt. He raises his arms to let me pull it off. He has amazing biceps, toned and muscly. His chest is hairless, but the main thing I notice is the paleness of his skin next to mine. I can't stop staring.

He gestures towards my purple top and asks me gently, "May I?"

I nod, and he pulls it over my head before dropping it over the side of the bed. I should feel exposed sitting there in my white bra facing him without my hijab on, but surprisingly I don't. It feels like the most natural thing in the world.

"Oh God, you're so gorgeous," he says, and then he pauses, as though unsure what to say or do next.

I lean into him again and this time when we push together, I kiss his neck, his skin, so hot under my lips it's like he has the same fire running through his veins. The feeling of skin on skin is exhilarating, the warmth, the closeness, how *right* it feels to be with him is what strikes me. Time stretches while we kiss, but eventually I stand and undo my bra hooks. Darren's eyes are wide, but I want this so bad.

He's suddenly still, like he doesn't want to move, except his breathing is laboured, and he doesn't take his eyes from me. Things are moving fast, but I do nothing to slow it down. I knew this was going to happen and, to be honest, I'm prepared for it.

He kisses me everywhere. I can't believe I'm allowing him to do this, but I am, and it feels amazing. I'm not going to let anything stop it, so when images of Mum and Dad and Shafqat Aunty appear in my mind, I squeeze my eyes shut and push them away.

"Are you sure you want to do this?" he asks me.

I nod. "I love you," I whisper. It feels so good to finally say it after all these months of suppressing my feelings. It's been so hard constantly holding back.

He stares at me and his face breaks into a tender smile. He gently puts his hand on my cheek. "I love you too."

I feel like a thousand fireworks have gone off in my mind. He loves me! My face aches from smiling, but then I notice that his expression has changed, a distracted look on his face.

"Oh shit!" he exclaims, making me jump. "I haven't got any . . ."

"Any?" I ask, impatiently.

"Condoms," he says. "I don't think I have any."

He gets out of bed and starts scrambling around, opening all the drawers in a desperate search. He ruffles his fingers through his hair. The mention of condoms makes me realise that we are actually going to do this. We've gone so far, and do I want to do this? Is it going to hurt? Will I bleed? Damn, I haven't brought any sanitary pads with me. What will it actually feel like?

"I don't suppose we can do it without can we?" All it takes is a look from him for me to get the message. "Yeah, that's stupid, sorry."

I gather my clothes from the floor and start putting on my bra. Does he have any idea what a big deal it is for me to even go this far?

"Wait, wait," he begs. "I'll just nip to the petrol station and get some. It's only five minutes away."

I hesitate. Is this a sign that we shouldn't be doing this?

"Please," he begs.

"Okay."

He pulls the T-shirt over his head. I don't think I've ever seen anyone dress this quickly.

"I'll be right back," he says. He kisses me on the lips and runs out of the door.

Once he's gone, I start putting my clothes on again; no way I'm just going to sit here topless. What if his dad comes back or something? I'm not sure what to do with myself while he's gone, and I start padding around his room looking at his things. There's not much to look at: some computer games, some pictures of him with his mum and a man I assume is his dad, and a few books. I run out of things to focus on until I see the Mac on his desk and decide to play some music; maybe filling the silence will make me feel better.

Standing by the computer, I catch sight of my reflection in Darren's mirror and am struck by how much I've changed since I met him. My hair is a tangled mess, my eyes seem so hard, all the deception seems to have made me look older. The enormity of what we are about to do suddenly hits me. Shafqat Aunty's sickly-sweet voice rings in my ears, "It's not me you will be disobeying, it is Allah."

Shafqat Aunty might not be here, but Allah is, and he sees everything. He sees what I am doing. This is wrong. What we are about to do is haram. Just because everyone else does it, doesn't mean it's right. We must fight the nafs. My body is tense, I'm staring at myself frozen in the mirror. I'm kidding myself thinking I can just separate myself from Islam when it's such a huge part of me, and if Darren is going to be with me, we have to get back on the right track.

CHAPTER THIRTY-EIGHT

The front door opens and Darren yells, "I'm back."

His footsteps thunder up the stairs. He's out of breath when he opens the bedroom door and I realise he must've run all the way. "I've got them," he says, holding up the box of condoms like it's a trophy.

I step back when he moves towards me.

"What?" he says, the smile fading from his face.

"I'm sorry, I can't do this," I say, and embarrassingly my eyes start to well up.

He chucks the packet of condoms on his bed.

"What's going on? Why are you giving me all these mixed messages? What is it that you want, Aisha?"

Tears run down my cheeks. My chest tightens to the point I fear it will crack, my sobs so loud even the neighbours must hear them. I feel so bad for doing this to him, mucking him around like this, but I cannot run from my faith.

Darren pales, a mixture of emotions flickering across his eyes. He walks toward me and hugs me tight. "Oh, Aisha, don't cry." He wipes my face with the sleeves of his hoodie. "You know you don't look good covered in snot." He laughs and it makes me smile. "Come and sit down, let's talk about this." I sit on his bed, and he puts his arms around me. "What's going on? Tell me what you're thinking."

I pause, take a deep breath, and say, "It's against my religion to have sex before marriage, and you not being a Muslim is a problem."

"What is it that you want me to say? I'm sixteen years old. I'm not thinking about marriage, and I'll be really honest with you, Aisha I don't want to be a Muslim."

My breath catches in my throat. "You don't?"

His eyes widen and he shakes his head at me. "I told you before, just because I'm mates with Muslims, it doesn't mean I want to be one."

"Well. . . why were you interested in my Ten Steps?" I ask.

He shrugs. "I dunno, I wanted to spend time with you and try to understand you more. I like you and I was open to learning more but . . ."

"But what?" I ask, my lips quivering.

"Look, don't take this the wrong way, but how can you expect me to convert to something that *you* seem really confused about?"

I hate that he said that to me, especially because I know that it's true.

He takes my hand in his. "You've got to decide what you want. If you want a relationship with me, I'm here waiting, but converting to Islam, I don't know, maybe it will happen in the future, but right now, I can't promise that it will." He squeezes my hand. "And there's something else."

"What?"

"At the end of this term, I'm moving back to London for Dad's job. . . he's finished his contract here."

I can't believe what I'm hearing. "What, you're moving away?"

He nods. "We can still see each other though."

He's moving away! I can't believe this. What am I going to do without him?

"How long have you known this?"

"A couple of weeks," he says.

"And you didn't tell me?" My chest hurts every time I breathe in like someone's squeezing it from inside.

"I'm sorry, I should have, I'm having a hard time dealing with it myself," he says. "I don't want to leave you."

Wiping my damp face with the sleeves of my top, I whisper, "I need to go home. I need to think things through."

"Okay," he replies. "Can I walk you home?"

"That's sweet but it's okay, I just need to go and clear my head."

The journey back is awful. The bus is packed, and I'm squashed from both sides and barely able to breathe. It doesn't help that I can still smell his aftershave on my skin. Whenever I think about us together the tears start again. He's right—I'm so confused. How can he leave me when we love each other? But then a voice in my head reminds me that he doesn't want to be a Muslim. I catch sight of my reflection in the window and my eyes are red and swollen.

When I get home, I'm surprised to see Isabelle leaving my house.

"Isabelle, what are you doing here? Were you looking for me?"

She smiles at me. "No, I just wanted to ask your mum something."

"What?" I ask. Since when does Isabelle want to ask Mum something? Isabelle has barely spoken two words to my mum the whole time I've known her. I doubt she even knows her name.

"How to make an egg and potato curry," she says slowly. Her voice has a strange, hard edge to it. "I've got to go now. Do thank your parents for the tea and samosas and say hi to your *boyfriend*." She practically slithers along the path and through the gate and is gone before I have a chance to ask any more questions.

CHAPTER THIRTY-NINE

Confused, I let myself in, and Mum and Dad are waiting in the hallway.

"Assalamualaikum," I say, my voice shaking.

"Wa-alaikum salam," Dad replies coldly. "Come into the sitting room, young lady. We need to talk to you."

I follow them, my legs weak; something bad has happened. When I enter the sitting room there's an eerie silence broken only by the sound of the clock ticking. I see a half-eaten samosa on the coffee table, and a cup with red lipstick marks on it. I assume it's Isabelle's leftovers until I see Shafqat Aunty sitting in the leather armchair in the corner that faces the TV.

"Aunty?" Has she said something?

"I just stopped by to see your mother." She smiles at me weakly, then drops her gaze.

The bitch has told them, I can't believe it! She found out somehow that I've still been seeing Darren and betrayed me! A cold shiver travels through my body. Did Isabelle say something? No, she wouldn't, she promised. But why was she here?

Mum and Dad motion for me to sit on the sofa, and they stand opposite me leaning against the fireplace. All three of them stare at me without speaking.

"Where are the boys?" I ask nervously, looking around.

"In their bedrooms. They will stay there until we finish talking to you." Dad's usual warmth is gone from his voice.

Mum still hasn't said anything. When I try to find her eyes, she looks in the other direction, as if she can't bear the sight of me.

"Where were you this afternoon?" Dad asks.

My brain starts working at a thousand miles an hour trying to come up with an excuse to get myself out of this mess.

"I was studying," I say.

Dad's face glowers and he paces back and forth. "I'll give you one more chance, Aisha, this time without lying—where were you?"

He must know about Darren, but if he already knows, why does he keep asking? Is it a trick question? What am I supposed to say?

"I-I was with a friend?" I flounder.

"Which friend?" He barks at me. "Your friend was just here."

"What—what did Isabelle say?" My lips quiver.

"She say you are with your boyfriend this afternoon!" Mum shouts. "Your *white* boyfriend. He's the same boy that you brought to the mela, isn't he?" Her eyes look as though they might pop out of her head. "Munafiq! You wear this hijab, and you lecture us about Islam, but behind our back you do all this—what kind of girl are you?"

The word 'Munafiq' rings in my ears because I know it means hypocrite—and it's true.

"She showed us on her phone your exact location," Dad says, answering the question before I even asked.

"What?" I gasp.

"Yes, on the Snapchats—it showed us where you were, and who you were with. She said this Darren boy is your boyfriend. Is it true, Aisha?"

My stomach drops through the floor. What do I say about Darren? Yes, he is my boyfriend but I'm not sure he can be anymore and Isabelle, why would she do this to me? To show them on Snapchat exactly where I was—that's just evil! So, it was Isabelle not Shafqat Aunty who betrayed me, but why is she here?

Isabelle's clearly been tracking me on her phone but wasn't she off all socials? She must have reactivated it in the last few days, after I told her about me and Darren. It all makes sense now, apart from why she would do this to me. I know we've had our ups and downs, but I really thought she was my friend. How many ways is my heart going to be broken today?

My chest feels tight and it's hard to breathe. The pain I felt earlier in Darren's room returns with full force, like a fist squeezing my chest to breaking point. The room starts spinning and I grab the edge of the sofa to steady myself.

"I don't feel well," I gasp. "Please—"

Mum rolls her eyes at me like I'm being a drama queen.

I try to calm myself down, but each breath feels sharp as knives. My hands tremble and my vision is blurred. What is happening to me? Shafqat Aunty gets up from the sofa and comes towards me.

"I think she's having a panic attack, let me pray some dua over her." She leans over me and recites one of our sacred prayers, the Ayat Al-Kursi, and the familiar Arabic words are soothing.

I don't know how long Shafqat Aunty is breathing over

me, but I finally feel my heartrate regulating, my breathing becoming more normal. She sits next to me and holds me in her arms, the smell of her as comforting as coming home.

"It will be okay, Aisha, Allah forgives everything. Take a deep breath and tell us what really happened." Her tone is soothing, and her soft warm arms keep me safe. I feel like I can breathe again. Despite everything she said, it wasn't her who betrayed me.

My parents sit opposite me. They don't look angry anymore, they just seem relieved that I'm not clutching at my chest.

The tears fall as I speak, "I'm sorry, it's true. I was at Darren's house today. We were just friends to start with, I promise. I thought I was in love with him, I really did—but one thing led to another and . . ." I hesitate. How much do I really have to tell them? I don't want to hurt them and all they know for certain is that I've been at his house—they don't have to know all the details.

"And what, Aisha?" Dad asks.

"We just kissed, that's all," I lie.

There's a collective sigh of relief.

"Subhanallah," Shafqat Aunty says. "Allah has protected you."

"You most certainly will not talk to that boy again," Dad says, standing. "If you see him at school, you are to avoid him, do you understand me? And you are not going anywhere in the evenings or weekends for a long time. If you need to study, you will study at home. You better make sure your results are good, young lady, is that clear?"

I nod and start crying again, but I know that I have got off lightly. I could have been sent to Pakistan.

"And you take off that hijab. It clearly means nothing to you," Mum hisses.

Shafqat Aunty takes Mum's hands. "Don't say that. I told you, Allah forgives, and we don't want Aisha to turn away from Islam because of one mistake. If she asks for forgiveness, this can all be forgotten."

Mum mumbles something that sounds like an agreement.

"Why don't you go and pray now?" Shafqat Aunty says to me.

I nod. Maybe praying will help; I've never needed Allah more. I head upstairs but halfway up, I can make out a few fragments of their conversation.

"Shafqat are you still going to Pakistan?" Dad asks.

"Yes, as soon as the summer holiday begins in a few weeks," she replies.

"Maybe I should come with you and bring Aisha."

My heart pounds and I go straight into the bathroom to start making wudu. The face in the mirror stares back at me all swollen and tear-stained. I don't think I've ever cried so much in one day. But now the tears have dried up, leaving my face tight, I know I don't want to be carted off to another country for good. I don't know anything about Pakistan. And what about my exams?

I go to the spare room and take my prayer mat and Qur'an and pray Asr. It's almost like being reunited with old friends. I beg Allah that my parents will forgive me and won't send me away. Unsurprisingly, Shafqat Aunty is right—I do feel better, but then I remember that Mum is right too: I am a hypocrite and a liar.

I don't even know who I am anymore.

CHAPTER FORTY

I greet Monday wide awake after a sleepless night. Dad confiscated my phone so I can't see my messages. He even found the burner phone Darren gave me. I had to sit there and watch him pull the sim out and lock it away in the safe. I didn't even bother to protest. Once Dad has made up his mind about something, nothing can change it. He can have a pathar ka dil—a heart of stone. I tried asking him about Pakistan, but he changed the subject. Maybe if I do well in the end of term exams he might soften? But how's that going to happen? The exams are in two weeks, and I've barely done any work all term.

The journey to school is a nightmare, my stomach is in knots when I think about Darren and how things are all up in the air with him. When I think about Isabelle, I just feel rage.

Chemistry is first thing, which means Darren will be there. When he sees me, he comes straight over before the lesson.

"Aisha, can we talk?" he asks, clueless as to what I've been through since we last saw each other.

I take my books out of my bag and place them on my desk. "I can't," I whisper. "Isabelle told my parents about us and I'm in really deep shit. This time they are threatening to ship me off to Pakistan for real."

His eyes widen. "Are you serious? Why did Isabelle do that? Do you want me to talk to her or maybe I should talk to your parents?"

"No, no, please you'll make it worse. Please don't say anything. I don't know why Isabelle did it, but I'm going to find out. Just go, we can't be seen together."

Darren lurks about after class wanting to talk to me again, but I shake my head at him. If Isabelle finds out she's just going to go and tell my parents and they'll ship me off sooner, maybe even before the end of term.

It's break-time and I'm desperate to find Isabelle. I want to punch her in the face, but I need to play this cleverly, get her on my side, be chalaaq, cunning, as Mum would say. The sixth form common room is jam-packed and it's hard to find her, but when I do, everything else fades away and all I can see is her. I dig my fingernails into my palms and count to ten before I go over. She's sitting with her friend Katy.

"Isabelle, we need to talk." I say firmly.

She looks me up and down. "So, talk."

"In private," I reply, jaw clenched.

"I'll go," Katy says, taking the hint.

"No, it's fine we can talk outside."

Isabelle rolls her eyes and follows me outside to the benches. "What's this about, Aisha?" she asks, curling her lip.

"You know what it's about—you told my parents about Darren! How could you do that to me?" I'm whispering but my words are rushed and I'm starting to feel short of breath. "Why did you do it? I thought we were friends!"

She shifts uncomfortably on the bench, and for a moment she looks almost sorry, but then she smirks again. "I didn't say anything."

"How can you deny it? I saw you leaving my house, Isabelle, for God's sake."

She rolls her eyes. "Okay, I told them, Aisha, I was worried about you."

"Why?"

"It's against your religion, having a boyfriend. I was just trying to protect you. To help you avoid hell and all that stuff."

Since when has Isabelle been interested in my faith?

"Couldn't you have come and talked to me then?"

"You were too into him," she says, brushing some imaginary lint from her jumper. "You wouldn't have listened."

There's something in her tone that sounds almost bored. I know she snitched on me deliberately and it has nothing to do with concern about me.

"I don't believe you," I say.

She leans towards me and spits, "You knew I liked Darren, but you went after him anyway. You stole him away and then you came to my house when I was already upset and rubbed it in my face—who do you think you are? You totally broke the girl code."

Is this how she saw it? How she sees *me*?

"And it was you, wasn't it? Putting all those anonymous messages on social media saying I was a slut? I can already see it now, high and mighty Aisha who never does anything bad looking down her nose at me."

"What? No! I would never do something like that!"

Isabelle looks me up and down. "Well who's the slut

now then, eh? Going around kissing boys and having boyfriends."

I shake my head at her in disbelief. "You've got it all wrong. I would never call you, or anyone else, anything like that. You know me, Isabelle, and I'm in no position to judge anyone. I really thought we were friends."

How could things have gone so wrong? I miss the friendship I had with Isabelle, how she helped me leave my comfort zone and tried to include me even when I made it difficult. And maybe she was right, and I hadn't been the best of friends getting involved with Darren, but what she did to me was unwarranted.

"Everything's ruined anyway. Last night I overheard my parents saying stuff about sending me to Pakistan."

"They. . . what? To Pakistan? I. . . shit!" She glanced around and her cheeks grew flushed. Eventually she turned back to me. "Look, I know I messed up, okay? I was angry and I wanted to do something to get back at you, but I didn't think it would get so serious. I'm sorry, Aisha. Do you want me to talk to your parents? Tell them I got it all wrong?" When the words leave her lips, so does her attitude.

"I don't think it will make any difference, just leave it." How can I even trust her now? Who knows what she might say next, and she might make the situation worse.

"I'm sorry," she repeats.

"I'm sorry too. . . for Darren."

"What's going to happen now with you two."

I sigh and tell her the truth. "I honestly don't know."

CHAPTER FORTY-ONE

After the rocky start, the rest of the week is spent in SPA—Studying, Praying, and Avoiding Darren, until I figure out what our next steps will be. Mum and Dad thaw gradually over the week. They no longer glare at me all the time, and no one mentions Pakistan, but there is a lot of praying and reading of Qur'an. My guess is they're hoping to purge my soul. Even if this week has felt as though someone has taken my heart and ripped it into a thousand pieces, the routine has helped. At least when I pray, I get some comfort—I beg God for forgiveness and hope that things will get better soon.

Although no one has said anything, Pakistan is still lingering over my head like a black cloud about to burst. I have to talk to my parents about it and find out what they're planning to do with me.

By Thursday night I finally feel brave enough to approach them. It's after dinner and I've finished washing up and made Mum and Dad a cup of tea to butter them up. They're sitting on the sofa in the kitchen.

As I pass Dad the tea, he gives me a gentle smile and says, "I know you are a good girl, Aisha."

"Then why send me to Pakistan?" I cry.

He shakes his head. "We are not, Aisha . . ." his words hang in the air.

"We think about it, about sending you for the summer, learn some discipline, some taqwa, but your Shafqat Aunty tell us not to," Mum explains.

"Shafqat Aunty?" I say, confused.

"She said that if we do that to you, you will hate us, and we will turn you more away from Allah," Dad says. "She said you are a good girl who made bad choices. I am sure she is correct."

I can't believe Shafqat Aunty stopped them from sending me away. Maybe there's still hope for our relationship.

By Friday, everything seems calmer, although it's been horrible seeing Darren around school and not being able to talk to him. I keep trying to think of a way for us to be together, but every road has a dead end. I always thought love conquers all, but how can it when there are so many roadblocks?

At the end of the school day when I open my locker, I find a letter with my name scrawled on top. I recognise his handwriting instantly and am in half a mind to open it then and there, but I decide to wait until I'm alone. It's not until the evening when I tear open the envelope and start reading. It's a list with a little note at the end.

Ten Things I Love About Aisha

1. *You're so clever.*
2. *You're passionate about your faith.*
3. *You're authentic and not afraid to admit that sometimes you're confused.*

4. *You make your own rules.*
5. *You're so brave.*
6. *You're sincere.*
7. *You're sweet and care about others enough to give up your whole weekend selling samosas.*
8. *You stand up to injustice.*
9. *You're so beautiful.*
10. *You're the only one I can talk to about my mum.*

I haven't been able to stop thinking about you since last weekend. It's been absolute torture being apart from you, seeing you and not being able to kiss you or talk to you.

When I said I love you, I meant it, and I'm sure you meant it too. It's made me realise I can't not be with you. I'm ready to be a Muslim if it means we can be together. I'm serious, I'll do anything to be with you.

Please talk to me—even if it's to say no. I'm leaving soon and I need to talk to you before I go. We can't end things like this.

Love, Darren x

OH MY GOD!

By the end of the weekend, I still have no idea what to do. Darren is serious about converting to Islam which is what I've wanted all along. Mum and Dad can't object if he becomes a Muslim. They might complain that he's white, but if he's a Muslim it would be wrong for them to not accept him. They can't. Let's face it, I've been obsessed with the guy since I first set eyes on him at the bus stop. All the slow afternoons I spent thinking about him, months desperately in love with him, and now he's telling me he feels the same way *and* he is willing to convert. Surely, there's only one answer to what he's suggesting?

I leave a note on Darren's desk on my way out of chemistry, asking him to meet me at lunchtime so we can talk. I don't stay long enough to watch him read it, but I hear his sigh of relief behind me.

The morning drags on and it seems like forever before lunchtime comes around and even longer before we can get our food and go outside and talk. I can't work out if I'm excited or dreading it.

We find a secluded space on the field and sit opposite each other. Ants are trailing across the ground nearby, and I spot one that's going in the wrong direction. I can totally relate.

"What did you think of my letter?" he asks nervously.

"I loved the list," I say, blushing. "I loved the end note too. I can't believe you're really moving away."

"You don't know how much it's cutting me up that I'm moving back to London and I won't see you every day."

What am I going to do once he's moved away?

"Did you mean what you said about converting to Islam?" I ask, hardly daring to breathe.

"Yeah, I know I skipped the rest of the steps, but. . . I do mean it."

"You do realise that if we do this properly, it means no sex before marriage?" If that doesn't test his determination, nothing will.

"I know," he says. "I'm prepared to do anything for us to be together, Aisha. I'll do anything to make you happy."

"But last time you said you didn't really want to be a Muslim. What's changed?"

"I want to be with you, and if converting to Islam is what it takes, then I'm willing to do it. It's been so painful being apart from you this week." He puts his hand on top of mine. "I love you."

It should be the happiest moment of my life—it's everything I've wanted. I should be over the moon, but instead my eyes fill with tears. I want so much to ignore the nagging feeling in my chest, but I can't.

CHAPTER FORTY-TWO

"But what if being with me wasn't a factor?" I ask. "Would you still want to be a Muslim?"

"I don't know," he shrugs. "If I'm really honest, I don't think it matters what religion you are—or even if you're any religion. Surely a kind God will let any decent person into heaven, won't He? Like my mum, for example."

I nod, I hear what he's saying, I really do. But I've realised over the past term that I cannot stop being a Muslim no matter what, that for me it goes far beyond just wearing the hijab or going to the mosque. I think even if I started drinking and eating bacon and sleeping with hundreds of men, it wouldn't change the fact that in my heart, I'm a Muslim through and through. Each time I've done something wrong, I always beg Allah for forgiveness, and I know he always does. I get comfort from praying to him. I can't change that—and I don't want to. I want someone who understands how important that is to me.

"I think what you're willing to do for me is so sweet, and I believe you when you say you love me—and I love you too, I really do. You know, when we met I wasn't looking for anything, but it's like you appeared from nowhere and you did something to me, to my heart. I didn't even know it was possible to feel like this about another human being."

Darren groans. "Why do I feel like a but is coming?"

I sigh. "But wanting to be with me is not a good enough reason to convert to Islam. You have to believe in it, and I just don't think that you do. You were right when you said I'm confused and need to work out what I want. I'm not the right person to bring you to the faith because I'm so conflicted about it myself." I pause for a moment. "Before, I thought that if you converted to Islam, it would solve everything, but I realise now I was just kidding myself."

"I thought that's what you wanted?"

"I did, but I realise now that I was wrong."

He stares at me, his face reflecting the pain I know he's feeling, because I feel it too.

"I was selfish, Darren. It was so wrong what I was trying to do."

"What do you mean?"

"I was trying to push you into becoming someone you're not, and that was wrong of me. I know that now because it's kind of what I did to myself. I was so desperate to fit in with either what Shafqat Aunty wanted or what I thought you wanted, and even who *I* thought I wanted to be, that I kind of lost myself."

"But I never pushed you, did I?" he asks quickly.

"No, that's not what I mean. I was so confused by either being what I thought was a perfect Muslim or being the ideal western girlfriend, that I didn't know who I was anymore. And, Darren, not knowing who you are is the most painful thing ever."

I've been so selfish; I realise that now.

He shakes his head and picks at the grass. "I don't blame you—you're caught between two worlds. But where does that leave us?"

"I can't believe I'm saying this, but I think that when you move away, that will be the end." My voice shakes as I say the words out loud. My chest feels tight and I squeeze my eyes shut, it hurts so badly.

"Can't we be friends?" he asks.

"I don't know if I can be your friend. I don't want to hear about who you're dating next; it would kill me."

I don't know if he's going back to his old school, and Shazya I'm sure will be snooping, but I don't dare ask. Just the thought of it makes my ribs ache.

"I can't believe this is it," he says.

"Me either," I whisper. "When are you moving back to London?"

"As soon as term is over, so two, three weeks. Is there nothing I can say that will make you change your mind?"

I shake my head, tears pouring down my face. I put my hand on his cheek and the familiar waves of electricity course through me.

"But I love you, Aisha," he says, his hazel eyes pooling with tears.

"I love you too," I whisper. This hurts. I screw my eyes up to rid myself of the pain. Soon I won't be able to touch him; he'll be gone, and I'll be alone again.

The end of term arrives quickly. Saying goodbye to Darren is the hardest thing I've ever done. I don't want to let go of him as he holds me tight, my tears soaking his shirt. I don't know what his dad knows about me, but he gives us time alone.

"Hey, don't cry," Darren says, wiping my tears. "We'll be in touch."

I nod and sniffle, trying to stop my nose from running. Will we still be able to talk as easily as we do now, or will it be different when we can't see each other? Will he still love me? I can't imagine loving anyone else the way I love Darren.

It's been a few days and the pain is still raw. It's so physical, under my ribs like someone is squeezing me. Sometimes I can't breathe from the pain. I'm numb and struggling to sleep, but when I do, I dream of him and wake with his name on my lips. Everything reminds me of him, whether it's walking past a Blitz or eating one of Mum's samosas. Even praying reminds me of Regent's Park Mosque and the way the sunlight brought out the amber flecks in his eyes. It's going to take a long time to get over this. I barely eat or sleep, and I feel sick all the time. My eyes are swollen from all the crying. Mum and Dad don't ask what's wrong; I think they already know.

I keep telling myself it's for the best and I'm going to get through this somehow. *It will pass, it will pass,* I repeat over and over like a mantra.

These feelings will go away but I don't know when. I don't regret meeting Darren though. Even though my heart is in ruins, maybe there are hidden treasures amongst the ruins. I'm not the same person I was before; I like to think that love has changed me for the better.

I've finally been allowed my phones back, and there are hundreds of messages left by Darren during that horrible week when we didn't speak to each other. I read and re-read them, savouring his pleas for me to meet him. My fingers hover over the keys and ignoring the way my heart skips, I delete his number, delete his Instagram, and throw the burner phone away. It's the only way I can move on and start to forget about him. I have to start afresh. I just want to stop thinking about him all the time.

There are also messages from Isabelle; she has been gracious enough to allow me some space, but still wants to know how I'm doing. I haven't responded, and I don't know if I will. This whole experience has made me realise that looking to others to make me feel whole isn't the answer. Can I really say I won't be tempted by another Darren further down the line? There will be boys I'll want to kiss before I get married, and I don't know if I can live up to my own standards. Isn't that where things went wrong for me in the first place?

I go into the bathroom and look in the mirror at the girl staring back at me: a sixteen-year-old with brown skin and wet eyes. I unpin and remove the material surrounding my head, set it aside, and run my fingers through my hair from front to back.

I stare at my hijab which looks so flimsy and insignificant next to the toothbrushes. Harmless. Picking it up, I hold it against my cheek. I'm thinking about the two baskets that I know are behind me.

The first is made of worn plastic and holds our family's dirty clothes while they wait their turn to be washed. The other is made of wicker, lined with a supermarket bag, and is emptied twice a week into the outside bin.

I look at the girl in the mirror once more as though to seek her advice, turn around, and make my choice.

ABOUT THE AUTHOR

Attiya Khan is a British Indian and grew up in Kent. She is a GP by profession and has three teenage children. She also holds an MA in modern Literature (with merit) from Birkbeck University and was longlisted for Undiscovered Voices 2020. She has had a number of articles published in medical journals and General Practice newspapers.

Attiya works as a GP in East London and is involved in medical education and training junior doctors. Her hobbies involve reading, writing and she is part of the Muslims women's cycling groups Joyriders and Cycle sisters which help keep her fit and happy.

Attiya identifies as a moderate Muslim and a feminist and is passionate about having the voices of BAME authors heard.